"You think we're really safe here?"

"I think I'll shoot first and ask questions later," Tyler said.

She smiled.

"You should think about going to the safe house," he told her quietly. "It's one thing for me to take chances with my life, but...I'm not so sure you should have that kind of faith in me."

"I have ultimate faith in you."

They exited the elevator. The hotel room door was barely closed, his gun and holster hurriedly laid by the bed before he had her in his arms, before they were both busy grasping at one another's clothing and dropping it all in a pile on the floor.

OUT OF THE DARKNESS

HEATHER GRAHAM

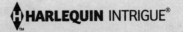

For Saxon and Joe,
two of the nicest and most talented young men I know.
May their move to New York be filled with dreams—
and, of course, all kinds of visits from West Coast friends!

ISBN-13: 978-1-335-52616-8

Out of the Darkness

Copyright © 2018 by Heather Graham Pozzessere

Recycling programs
for this product may
not exist in your area.

Printed in U.S.A.

New York Times and *USA TODAY* bestselling author **Heather Graham** has written more than a hundred novels. She's a winner of the Romance Writers of America's Lifetime Achievement Award, a Thriller Writers' Silver Bullet and, in 2016, the Thriller Master Award from ITS. She is an active member of International Thriller Writers and Mystery Writers of America, and is the founder of The Slush Pile Players, an author band and theatrical group. An avid scuba diver, ballroom dancer and mother of five, she still enjoys her South Florida home, but also loves to travel. For more information, check out her website, theoriginalheathergraham.com, or find Heather on Facebook.

Visit the Author Profile page at Harlequin.com.

Look for Heather Graham's next novel
A DANGEROUS GAME
available soon from MIRA Books.

CAST OF CHARACTERS

Sarah Hampton—The writer's quiet world is shattered when a murder reawakens the memories of a night she barely survived ten years ago.

Tyler Grant—This private investigator never stopped loving his high school sweetheart after trauma tore them apart.

Craig Frasier—FBI special agent in the New York City office.

Kieran Finnegan—Part-time pub owner, full-time psychologist who helps out on police and federal cases.

Davey Cray—Sarah's cousin.

Hannah Levine—Sarah's old high school friend who survived the massacre a decade ago.

Suzie Cornwall—Sarah's childhood best friend who also survived the attack.

Sean Avery—Another friend who survived that night.

Archibald Lemming—Escaped killer, dies after bloodbath.

Perry Knowlton—Escaped with Lemming; assumed dead at the hands of Lemming.

Robert (Bob) Green—NYPD homicide detective, worked the massacre as a young cop, and is the lead on the current murders.

Alex Morrison—Police photographer.

Dr. Lance Layton—Medical examiner.

Prologue

What Davey Knew

The Bronx
New York City, New York
Ten Years Ago

The eyes fell upon Sarah Hampton with a golden glow; the woman's mouth, covered with blood, split into a diabolical smile as she cackled with glee, raising her carving knife and slamming it down on the writhing man tied to the butcher block in the kitchen. Blood seemed to spurt everywhere. Screams rose.

And Sarah, laughing at herself for her own scream, grabbed Davey's hand and followed Tyler Grant out of the haunted house.

"Fun!" Tyler said, laughing, catching his breath.

It was fun. Though Sarah had to admit she was glad she was here as part of a party of six. Fun? Yes, sure...

And creepy! The weapons had looked real. The

"scare actors" could have passed for the real thing quite easily as far as she was concerned.

"Ah, come on, the guy on the butcher block—his screams were nowhere as good as they should have been," Hannah Levine said. "He must be getting tired of screaming—long season, long night. But I guess it is Halloween."

"Yeah, I imagine that the poor kid has been at it awhile," Sean Avery agreed. He looked at Sarah's cousin, Davey. "Then again, this place opens for only four weekends, with Halloween weekend, the last, being the boss. Coolest thing ever, Davey!"

Davey gave him a weird little half smile.

Suzie Cornwall—Sarah's best friend—frowned. "What's the matter, Davey? Was the haunted house too scary for you? We were all with you, you know."

"That one was okay," Davey said.

"But now…drumroll! We're moving on—to the major attraction!" Sean said.

"No, no, no!" Davey shook his head violently. "I'm scared!" He clearly didn't want to go into Cemetery Mansion, another of the haunted houses; he seemed terrified.

Sarah looked at her cousin with dismay.

She loved Davey. She really loved him. She had never met anyone who was as kind, as oblivious to what others thought, as willing to help others.

But Davey had Down syndrome. And while most of Sarah's friends were great, every once in a while they acted as if they didn't want to be with her, not if she was bringing Davey along.

And tonight…

Well, it was almost Halloween. And she and her friends had scored tickets to Haunted Hysteria in a radio contest. It was the prime event of the season, but one they couldn't actually afford. Well, to be honest—and they all had to agree—it was Davey who'd won the tickets. They'd asked him to dial the radio station number over and over again, and Davey hadn't minded.

The place itself was fabulous. Decorated to a T. Bats, ghouls, ghosts, vampires, witches and more—young actors and actresses, of course, but they walked around doing a brilliant job. The foam tombstones looked real and aged; the makeshift mortuary chapel was darkened as if older than time itself. Lights cast green and purple beams, and fog machines set in strategic places made for an absolutely immersive experience.

And now they were all here—she, Davey, Tyler, Sean, Suzie and Hannah. Suzie, tall and well-built, perfectly proportioned to be dressed up as Jessica Rabbit for the night, was her best friend. Tyler was the love of her life. And most of the time, both of them were truly wonderful friends. Tyler had even told her once that he knew right off the bat if he'd like people or not—all depending on the way they treated Davey.

Hannah was a stunner, olive skinned and dark haired—and as an evil fairy, she was even more exotically beautiful than usual. Sarah was pretty sure she'd caused one of the "scare actors" to pause—too startled by her beauty to scare her!

Sean…Sean was charming, the old class clown. Apropos, he was dressed up as the Joker. Every once in a while, his wit could be cruel. Mostly, though, he was a great guy, and the five of them had been friends forever, even though Sarah and Tyler were the only duo in their group.

She had come in steampunk apparel; Tyler had matched her with an amazing vest and frock coat. Davey had come as his all-time favorite personality—Elvis Presley.

They were all nearly eighteen now. Come October of next year, they'd be off at their different colleges, except she'd be at NYU with Tyler, as they'd planned. But for tonight…

It was fricking Halloween. Aunt Renee had asked her to take Davey with her. Yes, of course, Sarah was very aware the tickets really *belonged to Davey.*

Sarah always tried to be helpful. It was easy to help care for her cousin.

Aunt Renee wasn't in any kind of financial trouble—she had a great job as a buyer for a major chain store—and she had household help and could afford to send Davey to a special school.

But Aunt Renee wanted Davey to have friends and spend time with people his own age—Sarah's age. Aunt Renee wanted a wider world for Davey; she did not want his mom to be his only companion.

Sarah's friends were usually happy to have Davey with them.

But now Sarah could feel that Davey was holding them all back—and they were kids, with a right to be kids. The others were looking at her. Sure, they loved Davey. They were good people. But she could see them thinking *screw it!* They'd come to Haunted Hysteria; they were going in the haunted houses, and Sarah was welcome to sit outside with Davey.

Tyler, of course, had the grace to look guilty. He wasn't eighteen until January, but he was already over six foot three, heavily muscled in the shoulders and extremely fine in the face. Hot, yes. Tyler was hot. And he loved her. He really did. Then, she hoped she wasn't exactly dog chow herself. She was, she admitted, the typical cheerleader to his football hero. Yes, she was blonde and blue-eyed, the fault of her genetics. She was a good student and coordinated enough to be a great cheerleader. She liked to believe she'd been taught by her family to be a lot more, too—as in decent and compassionate and bright enough to see and understand others.

She thought Tyler was like that, too. No matter how cool he was.

They were just right for each other—and their group of friends was nice, too! Something she considered extremely important. Tonight, they wanted to be seniors—they wanted to be a little bit wicked and have a great time.

But being Davey's cousin had long ago taught Sarah about the importance of kindness in the world. Patience, sharing, caring…all that.

All that…

Seemed to go out the window right now.

"Davey, I know you were scared in the first house, but we're all with you," she said.

"Hey, buddy," Tyler told him. "I'm bigger than the damned ghosts!"

"You can go between Sarah and Tyler," Suzie said. "They'll protect you."

"No! No—the things in this house—they were okay. They weren't real. But that house...that one, there. There are things in it that are real. That are bad. They're evil!" Davey said.

"Oh, you're being silly," Hannah said.

"It's true," Davey said.

"How do you know?" Sean asked him.

"My father told me!" Davey said. "He helps me see."

Sarah bit her lip. Davey's dad had died over a year ago. Aunt Renee was alone with Davey now. Davey's dad had been a marine, and he had been killed serving his country. Her uncle had been a wonderful man—good to all the kids. She'd loved him, too, and she'd known he loved her.

"Davey, your father isn't here," she said. "You know...you know your dad is dead."

Davey looked at her stubbornly. "My father told me!" he insisted.

"Davey," Sarah said softly, calmly, "of course, the point is for it all to be very scary. Vampires, ghosts—but they're not real. It's a spooky fun place for Halloween. There are all kinds of made-up characters here."

"No. Real bad things."

They all let his words sit for a minute.

"The actors in there—they're not evil, Davey," Suzie said. "Come on, you've seen creatures like that before—and the ones who walk around, they're high school kids like us or college kids, and now and then, an adult actor without a show at the moment! You know all about actors, buddy. There are pretend vampires—and werewolves, mummies, ghosts—you name it."

"No. Not werewolves. Not vampires," Davey insisted. "Bad people. Like my dad said!"

"You love actors and movies," Sean said. Sean knew Davey had a skill for remembering everything about all the movies and, because of that, he always made sure Davey was on his team for trivia games. When they weren't playing trivia, however, Sean had a tendency to ignore Davey.

Sean seemed to be trying with the rest of their group to engage Davey, but he kept looking at his watch. He wanted to move on.

"You shouldn't go in! You shouldn't go in. It's bad. Very bad," Davey said.

"It's just a haunted house!" Tyler said.

"I love you, Tyler," Davey said. "Don't go. My father…he was next to me. Yes. He was next to me. All the things he taught me. He's dead, I know! But he's with me. He said not to go in. He said there would be bad men and you have to look out. He was smart. My dad was a marine!" he added proudly.

"That's kind of sick!" Hannah whispered to Sarah. "Does he honestly think…"

"Davey," Sarah said softly. "Your dad loved you—you loved your dad. But he's gone."

"I'm not going!" Davey said stubbornly.

"He should come," Tyler told Sarah. "If you give in to him all the time…it's not good. Don't make him into a baby. He's several years older than we are." He turned to Davey. "You know I love you, buddy, right?"

Davey nodded. "We don't have a weapon. I'm not going."

"Davey, I'm begging you…please?" Sarah asked.

Davey shook his head, looking at her. There were tears in his eyes; he was obviously afraid she was going to make him go into the haunted house.

"Just go," Sarah told the others. "Davey and I will get a soda or…hey, there are a bunch of movie toys over there. We'll go look at the toys."

Tyler sighed. "I'll stay with you."

The others had already fled like rats.

Not even Suzie—some best friend—stayed behind.

Just Tyler. Staring at her.

"Go," she told him, suddenly feeling put-upon.

"Sarah—"

"Go!"

He stiffened, squared his shoulder, shook his head—and walked on quickly to join the others.

"I'm still so confused. What scared you so badly?" Sarah asked Davey, leading him to a bench. At least she could sit. Her steampunk adventurer boots were starting to hurt like hell. "You were fine when we first got here. The haunted house we went in was made up to look like that one from the movie—you know, when the kids get lost in the woods and they find the house, but everyone in it is crazy! The father likes to hang people, the brother plays with a Civil War sword, the sister sprays poison and the mother chops up strangers for dinner. It was creepy cool—and they were all actors."

"Yes, they were actors," Davey said.

"Then why are you afraid of that one?" She pointed to the house where her friends were now in line, Cemetery Mansion. It was a good, creepy representation from a horror film where people had built over a graveyard and the dead came back to kill the living for disturbing them.

"It's evil," Davey said. He shoved his hands into his pockets and shivered. "I saw them. Dad told me to watch—I watched. That house is evil."

"How is it evil? It's honestly much the same. The themes are different. There are a lot of fabricated creatures—some cool motion-activated stuff, like robots—and then more actors. People just pretending. We went through the one house—it was fine."

He nodded very seriously and then pointed at the Cemetery Mansion.

"That one," he said. "It's wrong. I'm telling you, Sarah—it is wrong. And I like Tyler. And Suzie," he added. He didn't say anything about Sean or Hannah.

"You mean—you've heard they got the characters wrong somehow? We haven't been in it to see what the house is like, Davey."

"No, we can't go in," he said insistently, wetting his lips as he did when he got nervous. "No. It's wrong. You can feel it. It isn't scary—it's bad. Evil."

She looked at the house. It *was* spooky—the theme park had done a good job. Images were hazily visible in the windows: creatures that had just crawled from the grave, bony, warped, black-and-white, like zombies or ghosts, horrible to behold.

"You should stop your friends from going in there. Make Tyler come back. He wanted to stay with you. But you were all stubborn and mean."

Sarah heard the words and spun around to stare at Davey. But he didn't even seem to realize he had spoken to her.

He was looking at the stand where there were all kinds of toys.

Sarah suddenly smiled. His eyes were wide; he was happy to look at the toys. Davey loved the movies and he loved toys—that made movie-inspired props and toys extra special.

"Let's go see what they have," she told him.

"This is wrong," Tyler said as he got into the line for the haunted house with Suzie, Hannah and Sean. What was one more haunted house? he asked himself, irritated that he had let Sarah push him away. No matter if it was their idea or not, Davey had gotten them the tickets. He'd been patient enough to dial his phone over and over and over again.

And Tyler knew that Sarah was feeling alone—as

if Davey was her responsibility, and she wasn't about to burden anyone else.

Tyler loved her. He knew they were both lucky, both blessed. People referred to them as the "Barbie and Ken" of their school. He liked to think it wasn't just that he played football and she was an amazing cheerleader—for any team the school put forth. He tried to be friendly, kind, sympathetic—and he worked hard in class.

Naturally, he and Sarah had been intimate—though not in a way that would give others a chance to tease them. They were discreet and very private; Sarah would never do anything to disappoint her parents. But in their minds, marriage was a given. Sometimes, in the middle of a class, Tyler would smile, imagine being with her in such an intimate way again, when they both laughed, when they grew breathless, when the world seemed to explode. She was an amazing lover and he hoped he reciprocated. Sex was fireworks, but life was loving everything about her—her great compassion for others, her integrity. He liked to think that he was similar in his behavior.

Leaving her on her own tonight hadn't been considerate in any way.

"I'm going to go back and wait with Davey and Sarah," he said flatly.

"Go back where?" Hannah asked him. "They're already gone. And besides, Miss Stubborn Pride isn't going to let you stay with her. I'm sure you already tried to and she sent you after us. She doesn't want you to have a lousy time just because she has to."

Tyler gritted his teeth and looked away. "She isn't having a lousy time—and neither am I, Hannah. I love Davey. No one out there has a better heart."

It was true, though, that Sarah and Davey had walked off somewhere.

He should have firmly ignored Sarah when she'd pushed him away. She was usually bright enough to be angry if someone didn't understand that hanging out with Davey was like hanging out with any friend…

And Tyler was suddenly angry himself; they wouldn't be here at all without Davey. Davey had won the tickets.

"Oh, come on, Tyler!" Hannah said. "It's okay! The retard is *her* cousin, not yours."

He wanted to slap Hannah—and he was stunned by the intensity of the feeling. In his whole life, he'd never hit a girl. And Hannah was a friend. She was usually…fine.

"Hannah, you know calling him that is not okay. Not cool. He's just like you or me," Tyler said.

"Maybe like you!" Sean said, laughing. "Not me. Hey, come on—this is supposed to be the coolest thing here, ghosts coming up out of the ground from all over. They say the creatures—animatronic or whatever—are the most amazing, and they put their best 'scare' actors in this one. Tyler, come on, we take Davey with us all the time. But this is our night. It's our last Halloween together. If he doesn't want to come in, screw it!"

"Not to mention that, as I already pointed out,

we don't even know where they are anymore," Hannah said.

"Yep, well, I do have a cell phone," Tyler said.

"Tyler, leave it," Suzie said. She looked guilty, too, he thought. But maybe she was right. "We have VIP tickets—we get to move into the express lane up there. We'll be out soon and then we'll explore the food booths—Davey will like checking those out! And we'll hug him and tell him that he was right— we should have stayed out. It was really scary, so now we're all hungry!"

An actor in some kind of a zombie outfit came toward them, using a deep and hollow voice to ask for their tickets. They showed their passes and were moved up quickly in the line.

They entered the mudroom of the Cemetery Mansion. Bloody handprints were everywhere. They were met by a girl in a French maid outfit—with vampire teeth and blood dripping down her chin.

"Enter if you dare!" she said dramatically.

A terrified scream sounded from within. And then another. And another.

The place had to be amazingly good.

"Ah!" said the maid. "I say again, enter if you dare! Those who have come before you seem to be just… dying to get back out!"

She opened the door from the mudroom to the foyer and stepped back.

Tyler thought she looked concerned. As if…

As if people actually were dying to get out.

"CAN WE GO look at the booth over there?" Davey asked Sarah.

He gave her a smile that made her ashamed. She had been secretly bitter; she'd wanted to go with her friends. It wasn't terrible that she should want to; she knew her feelings were natural. But she felt guilty, anyway. Davey wasn't being mean, she knew. He wasn't hurting her on purpose. He had his irrational fear set in his mind.

"Come on!" She caught his hand and led him to the toy stand. This one was stocked with prop weapons.

There were all kinds of great things: realistic plastic ray guns, gold-gleaming light-up lasers and much more. There were fantastic swords, like from some 1950s sci-fi movie, she thought. They were really cool—silver and gold, and emitting light through plastic blades that shimmered in a dozen colors.

They were cheap, too. Not like the licensed merchandise. It was called a Martian Gamma Sword.

Sarah smiled, watching Davey's fascination.

She worked three days a week after school at the local theater and could easily afford the toy sci-fi sword. She paid while Davey was still playing with it.

"Okay, good to go," she told him.

He looked at her, surprised.

"I bought it, Davey. It's yours."

His eyes widened. He gave her his beautiful smile again. Then he frowned, appearing very thoughtful.

"Now we can go," he said.

"Pardon?"

"We have to go," he insisted. "I can save them now—Tyler and Suzie. I can save them."

Sarah couldn't have been more stunned. She smiled. Maybe they could catch up—and if not, well, she'd still be able to say she'd experienced the most terrifying haunted house in the city—the state, maybe even the country!

"Come on!" she said. "Sure, I mean, it will be great if we can save them. So great."

"I have to go first. I have the Martian Gamma Sword."

"Okay, I'm right behind you!" Sarah promised. She hurried after him.

"They don't like this kind of light, you know."

"Who doesn't like it?"

"Those who are evil!" he said seriously.

He had his sword ready and held in front of him—he was prepared, he was on guard!

Sarah smiled, keeping behind him. She hoped he didn't bat an actor over the head with the damned thing.

TYLER DIDN'T KNOW when it changed.

The haunted house was incredible, of course. He knew the decorations and fabrications, motion-activated creatures and the costumes for the live actors had been created by some of the finest designers in the movie world.

The foyer had the necessary spiderwebs dangling from the chandelier and hanging about. As they were ushered in—the door shut behind them by the French maid—a butler appeared. He was skinny, tiny and a hunchback. Igor? He spoke with a deep voice that was absolutely chilling.

Tyler had to remind himself he was six-three and two hundred and twenty pounds of muscle. But just the guy's voice was creepy as hell.

"Cemetery Mansion!" the butler boomed out. "The living are always ever so careless of the dead! Housing is needed…and cemeteries are ignored. And so it was when the Stuart family came to Crow Corners. They saw the gravestones…they even knew the chapel housed the dead and that a crypt led far beneath the ground. And still! They tossed aside the gravestones, and they built their mansion. Little did they know they would pay for their total disregard. Oh, Lord, they would pay! They would be allowed to stay—forever! Forever and ever…with those who resided here already!"

Suddenly, from thin air, haunts and ghouls seemed to arise and sweep through the room. Suzie let out a squeal. Even Hannah shrieked.

Good old Sean let out a startled scream and then began to laugh at himself.

It was done with projectors, Tyler realized.

"To your left, ladies and gentlemen, to your left! The music room, and then the dining room!"

They were urged to move on. The music room hosted a piano and rich Victorian furniture. There was also a child sitting on the sofa, holding a teddy bear. She turned to look at them with soulless eyes— and then she disappeared. A figure was hunched over the piano. Suzie tried to walk by it; the piano player suddenly stood, reaching out for her.

She screamed. The thing was a motion-activated figure, one who would have done any haunted mansion proud. It was a tall butler—blond and grim-looking, with a striking face made up so that the cheeks were entirely hollow. It spoke with a mechanical voice. "Come closer, come closer... I can love you into eternity!"

It was nothing but a prop, an automaton. But it was real as all hell.

Suzie ran on into the next room.

The dining room...

At the head of the table was a very tall man—an actor portraying the long-dead head of the household; a man in a Victorian-era suit, wearing tons of makeup that had been applied very effectively. He was sharpening a knife.

There were dummies or mannequins or maybe animatronics slumped around the table. At least their bodies were slumped there. Their heads were *on* it. Blood streamed from their necks and down their costumes.

"One of them is going to hop up, I know," Hannah murmured.

She bravely stepped closer to the table. No one moved.

Tyler noticed there was a girl about their age at the end of the table. She was wearing one of this year's passes to Haunted Hysteria around the stump of her neck.

Good touch, he thought.

The bodies around the table did not move. The master of the house watched them with bloodshot eyes. He sharpened his knife.

A girl suddenly burst into the dining room from the music room. "Run! Get out—get to the exit! He's in the house somewhere!" she screamed.

"Yes, he is. He's right here," the master of the house said. He reached for her and dragged her to him. She screamed again, trying to wrench herself free. He smiled.

He took one of the knives he had been sharpening.

And he slit her throat.

SARAH DIDN'T KNOW what had gotten into Davey; he was usually the most polite person in the world. He'd been taught the importance of *please* and *thank you*.

But he was almost pushing.

And he knew their radio station tickets gave them VIP status.

Light sword held before him, he made his way to one of the actors herding the line. "VIP, please!" he told her.

"Uh, sure. Watch out for that thing!" She started to lead them up the line, toward the house. As she did so, there was a scream, and one of the actors came bursting out the front door.

She was dressed as a French maid—a vampire or zombie French maid, Sarah thought.

She stumbled out of the entry and onto the porch,

grabbing for one of the columns. Blood was dripping down her arms and over her shirt—she appeared to have a number of stab wounds.

"Don't!" she shouted. "Don't... He's a killer!"

Applause broke out in the line. But then someone else burst out of the house—a ghoul dressed in an Edwardian jacket.

He crashed down, a pool of blood forming right on the porch.

More applause broke out.

"No, no, that's not supposed to happen," the zombie leading Sarah up the line murmured.

Davey burst by her; he was headed to the house, his light saber before him.

"Davey!" Sarah shrieked. Something was wrong; something was truly wrong. They needed to stay out, needed to find out if this was an excellent piece of play-acting or...

Or what?

Imaginary creatures came to life and started killing people? Actors went crazy en masse and started knifing the populace? Whatever was going on, it seemed insane!

The sensation that crawled over Sarah then was nothing short of absolute terror—but Davey was ahead of her.

With his Martian Gamma Sword.

He was charging toward the house.

Davey! She had to follow him, stop him and get him away—no matter what!

TYLER COULD HEAR nothing but diabolical laughter.

And screaming—terrified shrieks!

Suzie hopped on a chair and grabbed a serving platter for defense.

The master of the house turned toward them, dropping the body of the girl whose throat he had slit. It fell with a flat thud.

Sean squeaked out a sound that was nearly a scream.

Hannah grabbed Sean, thrusting him between her and the big man with the massive knife.

"Back up, back up, back up!" Tyler said.

Hannah did so. Sean turned to flee.

The master of the house went for Sean. He picked him up by the neck.

"No! Stop, stop it!" Tyler shouted.

This couldn't be happening.

"This isn't funny. It isn't right!"

The character didn't seem to hear Tyler. And Tyler had no choice. He leaped forward, shoving Hannah away, and tried to wrest Sean from the killer. He grabbed Sean's arm and pulled.

"No!" Suzie shrieked.

Tyler looked up.

The master of the house was approaching her with the massive knife, dragging Sean along with him. Then he turned. He came swinging toward Tyler, still dragging Sean. Tyler held on to his friend and jerked hard; Sean came free and they staggered back— Hannah, Sean and himself—until they crashed into the table.

Hannah began shrieking in earnest. As she did so, Tyler became aware of the tinny scent of blood.

Real blood.

And he looked around the table and he knew.

They were people. Real people. And they were dead.

Really dead.

"No!" Suzie shrieked.

She slammed her serving platter at the master of the house.

He just laughed.

And raised his carving knife.

DAVEY RACED ACROSS the porch, pushing aside the bleeding maid and hopping over the body of the man in the Edwardian dress.

Sarah had no choice but to follow.

He burst through into a mudroom. There were bloody handprints all over it.

Some were fake—stage blood.

Some were real—human blood.

She could tell by the smell that some of the blood was real.

Davey rushed through to the foyer, his Martian Gamma Sword leading the way. But there was no one there. He threw open another door.

"Davey, stop! Please, Davey, something is going wrong. Something is…"

They were in a music room; it was empty—other than for a bloody body stretched across a floral sofa.

"Davey!" Sarah shrieked. "No, no, please…"

She started to whirl around. There were holograms everywhere. A child in black with a headless doll appeared. And then a hanged man, the noose still around his neck. All kinds of ghouls and creatures and evil beings began to appear in the room and then disappear.

"Davey, please, we've got to get out. Davey!"

She gripped his arm as the terrifying images swirled around them.

"Not real," Davey said. "Sarah, they're not real."

He was moving on—and she heard screams again. Terrified screams...

He went through a black hazy curtain and they were in the dining room.

And there were Tyler, Hannah...Sean and Suzie... It appeared that they were all being attacked by...a creature, by someone or something. They had fallen back and were struggling to rise from the dining table, where there were...

Oh, God, corpses, real corpses. Dead people, all around the table. Suzie and Hannah were yelling and screaming, and Tyler was reaching out, but the carving knife was coming down and it was going to sink into Tyler's chest at any minute!

She heard a terrible scream—high-pitched and full of fear and horror. And she realized it was coming from her...

And she had drawn the attention of the...

Man. It was a real man.

An actor gone insane? What the hell?

No, no, no, no. It was impossible. It was Halloween. It had to be a prank, an elaborate show…

The man was real.

Absolutely real.

He was tall and big and had long scraggly white hair and he might have played a maniacal killer in a slasher movie.

Except this wasn't a movie.

And he was coming at her.

He opened his mouth and smiled, and she saw his fangs. Long fangs that seemed to drip with something red…stage blood…

Real blood.

She screamed again.

It sounded as if it was coming from someone else, but it was not. It was coming from her.

Tyler struggled up from the table. He slipped.

He was slipping in blood.

"No, no, no!" Sarah screamed.

And then Davey stepped up. He thrust her back with his arm and stepped before her, his cheap little plastic sword at the ready.

"Leave her!" Davey shouted, his voice filled with command.

The man laughed…

And Davey struck him. Struck him hard, with all his strength.

The man went flying back. He slammed into the wall, and the impact sent him flying forward once again.

He tripped on a dead girl's leg…

And crashed down on the table.

Right on top of Tyler and Sean and Hannah, who had already been slammed down there. It was too much weight. The table broke with an awful groaning and splintering sound.

Shards and pieces flew everywhere as what remained of the table totally upended.

Tyler let out a cry of fear and fury and gripped the man's shoulders, shoving him off with all the force of a high school quarterback.

To Sarah's astonishment, the man, balanced for a matter of seconds, staring furiously at Davey—and then he fell hard. And didn't move again. She saw that he'd fallen on a broken and jagged leg of the table.

The splintered shaft was sticking straight through his chest.

Tyler got up and hunkered down by the man carefully, using one of the plates off the table as a shield.

"Dead," he said incredulously. He looked up at the others. "He's dead... He fell on the broken table leg there and...oh, God, it's bad."

"Out of here! It's evil!" Davey commanded. "It's still evil."

They were all shaking so badly no one seemed able to move. Davey reached for Hannah's arm and pulled her up. "Out!" he commanded.

And she ran. Suzie followed her, and then Sean, and then Tyler met Sarah's eyes and took her hand, and they raced out, as well, followed by Davey—who was still carefully wielding his plastic sword.

They heard sirens; police and security and EMTs were spilling onto the grounds.

The medics were struggling, trying to find the injured *people* among the props and corpses and demons and clowns.

When the group of friends reached a grassy spot, Sarah fell to the ground, shaking. She looked up at Davey, still not beginning to comprehend how he had known…

Or even *what* it was he had known.

"I told you—that house is evil," he said. "I told you—my dad. He taught me to watch. He stays with me and tells me to watch."

IT HAD BEEN the unthinkable—or easily thinkable, really, in the midst of all that went on at a horror-themed attraction at Halloween.

Archibald Lemming and another inmate had escaped from state prison two weeks earlier. They had gotten out through the infirmary—even though he had been in maximum security. News of the breakout had been harried and spotty, and most people assumed the embarrassment suffered by those who had let them escape had mandated that the information about it be kept secret.

Archibald Lemming had been incarcerated at the Clinton Correction Facility for killing four people—with a carving knife. The man had been incredibly sick. He'd somehow managed to consume some of the blood in their bodies—*as if he'd been a damned vampire.* He'd escaped with a fellow inmate, another killer who was adept with a knife and liked to play in blood—Perry Knowlton. Apparently, however, Lemming had turned on the man. Knowlton's body had been found burned to little more than cinders in the crematorium at an abandoned veterinary hospital just outside the massive walls of the prison.

Sarah knew all that, of course, because it was on the news. And because, after the attack at Cemetery Mansion, the cops came to talk to her and Davey several times. One of them was a very old detective named Mark Holiday. He was gentle. His partner, Bob Green, was younger and persistent, but when his questions threatened to upset Davey, Sarah learned she could be very fierce herself. The police photographer, Alex Morrison—a nice guy, with the forensic unit—came with the detectives. He showed them pictures that caused them to relive the event—and remember it bit by bit. The photographer was young, like Bob Green. He tried to make things easier, too, by explaining all that he could.

"Archibald Lemming! They found his stash in prison. Idiot kept 'history' books. Right—they were on the Countess Bathory, the Hungarian broad who killed young women to bathe in their blood. The man was beyond depraved," one of the cops had said that night when he'd met with the kids. He'd been shaking, just as they had been.

People were stunned and angry—furious. If there had been better information on the escape, lives might have been saved. Before the confrontation with Davey and his friends, the man had killed ten people and seriously injured many more. He'd managed to escape at a time when it was perfect to practice his horror upon others—Halloween. He had dressed up and slipped into the park as one of the actors.

But many survived who might have died that night. They had lived because of Davey.

It did something to them all. Maybe they were in shock. Maybe denial. Guilt over being the ones who made it out. And confusion over what it meant, now that the normal lives ahead of them seemed all the more precious.

Sarah was with her cousin and her aunt when Tyler came to say goodbye.

He was leaving the school, going into a military academy and joining the navy as soon as he could.

Sarah was stunned. But in an odd way, she understood. She knew she had closed in on herself. Maybe they all had, and needed to do so in order to process that they were alive—and it was all right for them to go on.

She, Tyler and their friends had survived. And it was too hard to be together. Too hard to be reminded what the haunted house had looked like with all the dead bodies and the blood and things so horrible they almost couldn't be believed.

So she merely nodded when he told her he was leaving. She barely even kissed him goodbye, although there was a long moment when they looked at each other, and even *this*—losing one another—was something they both accepted, and shared, and understood.

Sarah gave up cheerleading and transferred to a private school herself, somewhere that hadn't lost any students in the Cemetery Mansion massacre.

When college rolled around, she decided on Columbia and majored in creative writing, veering away from anything that had to do with mystery or horror. She chose a pseudonym and started out in romance.

However, romance eluded her. She was haunted by the past.

And by memories of Tyler.

She turned to science fiction.

Giant bugs on the moon didn't scare her.

Except...

Every once in a while, she would pause, stare out the window and remember she was alive because of Davey and his Martian Gamma Sword.

Still, by the time she was twenty-seven, she was doing well. She had her own apartment on Reed Street. For holidays she headed out to LA—her parents had moved there as soon as her dad had retired from his job as an investment banker. Of course, they always tried to get her to join them with a permanent move, but she was a New Yorker and she loved the city. Sometimes she guest-lectured at Columbia or NYU. Upon occasion, she dated. Nothing seemed to work very well. But she was okay. She had college friends, and since she'd worked her way through school waitressing at an Irish pub, she still went in to help out at Finnegan's on Broadway now and then. The Finnegan family were great friends—especially Kieran, who happened to be a psychologist who frequently worked with criminals. He always seemed to know when Sarah wanted to talk a little about what she'd been through—and when she didn't.

It wasn't the happiness she had envisioned for herself before the night at the Halloween attraction.

But it was okay.

She hadn't seen Tyler—or any of her old friends—for over a decade.

Sarah had been living in the present.

And then she heard about the murder of Hannah Levine.

Like it or not, the past came crashing down on her.

And with it, Tyler Grant reentered her life.

Chapter One

"Tyler!"

Davey Cray greeted Tyler with a smile like no other. He stepped forward instantly, no hesitation after ten years—just a greeting fueled by pure love.

It was as if he had expected him. Maybe he had.

Tyler hugged Davey in return, a wealth of emotions flooding through him.

"I knew you'd come. I knew you'd come!" Davey said. "My mom said you were busy, you didn't live here anymore. You work in Boston. But I knew you would come." His smile faded. "You came for Hannah." Davey looked perplexed. "Hannah wasn't always very nice. And I watched the news. She wasn't doing good things. But…poor Hannah. Poor Hannah."

Yes, poor Hannah. She'd disappeared after leaving a bar near Times Square.

Her torso and limbs had turned up on a bank of the Hudson River.

Her head had come up just downriver about a half mile. She had been savagely cut to ribbons, much like the victims ten years past.

According to the news, Hannah had become a bartender, and then a stripper—and then a cocaine addict. Had that already been in the cards for her? Or had her life been twisted on that horrible night?

"Poor Hannah, yes. Nobody deserves to have their life stolen," Tyler assured Davey. "Nobody," he repeated firmly. "Had you—seen her?"

Davey shook his head gravely. "My mom doesn't let me go to strip clubs!" he said, almost in a whisper. Then he smiled again. "Tyler, I have a girlfriend. She has Down syndrome like me."

"Well, wow! That's cool. Got a picture?"

Davey did. He pulled out his wallet. He showed Tyler a picture of a lovely young girl with a smile as magnificent as his, short brown hair and big brown eyes.

"She's a looker!" Tyler said.

"Megan. Her name is Megan." Davey grinned happily.

"That's wonderful."

"Sarah set me up on the right kind of page on the internet. It really is cool."

"I'll bet it is! Leave it to Sarah."

"She loves me. And, you know, she loves you, too."

"Of course. We all love each other."

By that time, Renee Cray had made it to the door. She was a tall, thin, blonde woman in her late forties, with big brown eyes just like Davey's. "Tyler!" she exclaimed.

And then she, too, threw her arms around him,

as if he was the lost black sheep of the family being welcomed back into the fold.

Maybe he was.

"Tyler! How wonderful to see you! We knew, of course, that you'd joined the navy. And I know Sarah had heard you're living in Boston, working there as some kind of a consultant. Police consultant? PI? Something like that?"

"Exactly like that," he told her.

Renee continued to stare at him. "You're here… because of Hannah Levine, right? But…what can you do? What can anyone do? Is it horrible to say I'm glad her parents died in a car accident years ago? But what…" Her voice trailed off, and then she straightened. "Where are my manners? Come in, come in—you know the way, of course!"

He entered the parlor; Renee and Davey lived in a charming little two-story house in Brooklyn that offered a real yard and a porch with several rocking chairs. Renee was a buyer for a major retail chain and was able to keep up a very nice home on her own salary. Since the death of her husband, she had never done much more than work—and care for Davey. Tyler doubted she had changed. She was, in his opinion, a wonderful mother, never making Davey too dependent and never becoming codependent herself.

"Sit, sit," Renee told him. "Davey, get Tyler some tea, will you, please? You still like iced tea, right?"

"Still love it," Tyler assured her.

When her son was gone, Renee leaned forward. "Oh, Tyler! It's been so hard to listen to the news. I

mean, bad things happen all the time. It's just that…
you all escaped such a terrible thing, and now Hannah. Of course, her lifestyle…but then again, no one
asks to be murdered… They haven't given out many
details. We don't know if she was raped and murdered, but she was…decapitated. Beheaded. Just
like—"

She broke off again, shaking her head. "It's like
it's the same killer—as if he came back. Oh, I'll never
forget that night! Hearing what had happened, trying to find Davey, trying to find you children… Oh,
Tyler! Hannah now…it's just too sad!"

"It's not the same killer," Tyler said quietly. "I saw
Archibald Lemming die. I saw him with a wooden
table leg sticking straight through him. He did not miraculously get up and come back to kill again. Hannah had demons she dealt with, but they were in the
way she looked at life. It's tragic, because no one
should ever die like that. And," he reflected softly,
"she was our friend. We were all friends back then.
We haven't seen each other in a while, but…we were
friends. We knew her."

Renee nodded, still visibly shaken.

Maybe they hadn't seen Hannah in a long time,
but she had still been one of them.

"Tyler, I guess it's been in the media everywhere,
but…you weren't that close with Hannah, were you?
Had you talked to her? How did you come to be
here?"

He smiled grimly.

Sarah. Sarah was why he had come. He thought

back, hardly twelve hours earlier, when he had heard from her. He had received the text message from an unknown number.

Hi Tyler. It's Sarah. Have you seen the news?

Yes, of course he'd seen the news.

And he'd been saddened and shocked. He'd been there the night of one of the most gruesome spree killings in American history, and then he'd gone on to war. Not much compared to the atrocities one could see in battle. Between the two, he was a fairly hardened man.

But...their old friend Hannah had been brutally murdered. And even if her life had taken a turn for the worse lately—which the media was playing up—neither she, nor any victim, should ever have to suffer such horrors.

While Tyler hadn't seen Sarah in a decade, the second he received the missive from her, it felt as if lightning bolts tore straight through his middle and out through every extremity.

They said time healed all wounds. He wasn't so sure. He never really understood why he'd done what he'd done himself, except that, in the midst of the trauma and turmoil that had swept around them that night in a long-gone October, Sarah had still seemed to push him away. She always said she was fine, absolutely fine. That she needed to worry about Davey.

She had rejected Tyler's help—just as she had refused to understand he'd been willing to make Davey his responsibility, just as much as Davey was Sarah's responsibility.

They'd all had to deal with what had happened, with what they had witnessed.

Tyler had always wanted her to know he loved Davey, and he never minded responsibility, and he didn't give a damn about anyone else's thoughts or opinions on the matter. They had to allow Davey a certain freedom. When they were with him, they both needed to be responsible. That was sharing life, and it was certainly no burden to Tyler.

But Sarah had shut down; she had found excuses not to see him.

And he'd had to leave.

Maybe, after that, pride had taken hold. She had never tried to reach him.

And so he had never tried to get in touch with her.

But now...

Now Sarah had reached out to him.

He'd kept up with information about her, of course. Easy enough; she kept a professional platform going.

He liked to think she had followed him, as well. Not that he was as forthcoming about where he was and what he was doing. He had become a licensed investigator and consultant. Most of his work had been with the Boston Police Department; some had been with the FBI.

He knew she hadn't gone far. Her parents had rented out their Brooklyn home and moved to California. Sarah was living in Manhattan. She'd found a successful career writing fiction—he'd bought her books, naturally. Her early romances reminded him of the two of them; they'd been so young when they'd been together, so idealistic. They'd believed in humanity and the world and that all good things were possible.

Her sci-fi novels were fun—filled with cool creatures, "aliens" who seemed to parallel real life, and bits of sound science.

Part of why he'd never tried to contact her again had been pride, yes. Part of his efforts had actually been almost noble—her life looked good; he didn't want to ruin it.

But now…

Yes, he'd seen the news. Hannah Levine had been murdered. The reporters had not dealt gently with the victim because of her lifestyle. They hadn't known her. Hadn't known how poor she'd grown up, and that she had lost both parents tragically to an accident on the FDR. They did mention, briefly, that she'd survived the night of horror long ago.

As if reading his mind, Renee said, "They're almost acting as if she deserved it, Tyler! Deserved it, because of the way she lived. I'm wishing I had tried harder. Oh, look! If she hadn't been an 'escort,' this wouldn't have happened to her. I feel terrible. I mean, who ever really understands what makes us tick? Not even shrinks! Because…well, poor child, poor child! She never had much—that father of hers was a blowhard, but he was her dad. Both dead, no help…and she was a beautiful little thing. She was probably a very good stripper."

That almost made Tyler smile. "Probably," he agreed. "And yes, she was beautiful. Have the police let anything else out yet?"

"We know what you know. Her body was found… and then a few hours later, her head was found. First, we heard about the body in the river. Then we heard that it was Hannah."

The front door opened and closed. Tyler felt that same streak of electricity tear through him; he knew Sarah was there.

Renee frowned. "Sarah must be here."

"I'm sorry. I should have said right off the bat that she was meeting me here," Tyler said. "That's why… why I came. She didn't tell you?"

"No, but…that's great. You've been talking to Sarah!" Renee clapped her hands together, appearing ecstatic.

"We've exchanged two sentences, Renee," he said quietly. "Sorry, four sentences, really. 'Did you hear the news?' 'Yes.' 'Will you come and meet me at Aunt Renee's?' And then, 'Yes, I'll come right away.'"

Renee just nodded. Davey was coming back in the room, bearing glasses of iced tea. "Sarah is here," Renee said.

Davey nodded gravely. "Of course she is."

Tyler watched as she walked into the parlor. Sarah. Whom he hadn't seen in a decade. She hadn't changed at all. She had changed incredibly. There was nothing of the child left in her. Her facial lines had sharpened into exquisite detail. She had matured naturally and beautifully, all the soft edges of extreme youth falling away to leave an elegantly cast blue-eyed beauty there, as if a picture had come into sharp focus. She was wearing her hair at shoulder length; it had darkened a little, into a deep sun-touched honey color.

He stood. She was staring at him in turn.

Seeing what kind of a difference a decade made.

"Hey," he said softly.

"Hey!" she replied.

They were both awkward, to say the least. She started to move forward quickly—the natural inclination to hug someone you held dear and hadn't seen in a long time.

He did the same.

She stopped.

He stopped.

Then they both smiled, and laughed, and she stepped forward into his arms.

It was impossible, of course. Impossible that they had really known what the depths of love could be when they hadn't even been eighteen. Then he'd felt as if he'd known, right from the first time he'd seen her at school, that he loved her. Would always love her.

That no one could compare.

And now, holding her again, he knew why nothing had ever worked for him. He'd met so many women— lots of them bright, beautiful and wonderful—and yet nothing had ever become more than brief moments of enjoyment, of gentle caring, and never this…connection.

Sarah had called on him because a friend had been murdered, and he was the only one who could really understand just what it was like. This didn't change anything; whether he loved her or not, she would still be determined to push him away when it came to relying on him, sharing with him…

Back then, she hadn't even wanted him near.

They drew apart. It felt as if the clean scent of her shampoo and the delicate, haunting allure of her fragrance lingered, a sweet and poignant memory all around him.

"You are here," she said. "Thanks. I know this is crazy, but…Hannah. To have survived what happened that October, and then…have this happen. I understand you're in some kind of law enforcement."

"No. Private investigator. That's why I'm not so sure how I can really be of help here."

"Private investigators get to—investigate, right?" Sarah asked.

"Why don't you two sit down?" Renee suggested.

"Sit, sit. Have tea!" Davey said happily.

Once again, Tyler sat. For a moment, the room was still, and everyone in it seemed to feel very awkward.

"I'm glad you came," Sarah said. "Not that I really know anything. I belong to a great writers' group that brings us down to the FBI offices once a year for research, but…I really don't know anything. I don't think the FBI is involved. New York police, high-crimes or whatever they call it division… I just— The killing…sounds way too familiar!"

Tyler nodded. "Yeah. Though psychopaths have beheaded and sliced up victims many times, I'm sorry to say. And, of course," he said, pausing then to take a breath, "well, we were there. We saw the killer die back then." He looked over at Davey and smiled tightly, still curious about how Davey had sensed so much of what had gone on. "We were all there. We saw him die. Davey was a hero."

"My dad. My dad was with me," Davey said.

"In all he taught you, and all you learned so well!" Renee said, looking at her son, her soft tone filled with pain for the husband she'd lost.

"The police may already have something," Tyler said. "When a murder like this occurs, they hold back details from the press. You wouldn't believe the number of crazy people who will call in and confess to something they didn't do, wanting what they see as the credit for such a heinous crime. I have friends in Boston who have friends in New York. Maybe I can help—all depends on whether they want to let me in or not."

"Sarah has friends, too!" Davey said.

Sarah looked at him. "I do?"

"Kieran!"

"I haven't talked to her in a while," Sarah murmured.

"Who is Kieran?" Tyler asked.

"A friend, yes," Sarah said, looking at him. "She and her brothers inherited a very old Irish pub on Broadway—downtown, near Trinity and St. Paul's. The oldest brother manages, Kieran works there sometimes."

"You worked there!" Davey said.

"I did—I worked there through college," Sarah

said. "Anyway, Kieran is a psychologist who works with two psychiatrists, Drs. Fuller and Miro. They often work with the police—they're geniuses when it comes to the criminal psyche. And her boyfriend is a special agent with the FBI. So, yes, if I asked for help…"

"That's excellent," Tyler told her. "And it could really help, as far as finding out whatever information there is forthcoming. Other than that… I'm not law enforcement."

"But people hire PIs all the time," Renee said.

"When someone is missing, the family might hire someone. In murder investigations that go cold…"

"We can hire you!" Davey said happily.

"We're not her family," Sarah said.

"That doesn't matter. We were her friends," Davey said. He was quiet a minute and made one of his little frowns. "She was mean to me sometimes, but she was my friend, too. Mostly she was nice to me."

They all fell silent.

"I'll figure something out, and I'll keep you posted. I do have a legal standing as a private investigator, but it's a lot nicer if the police want me involved."

Sarah nodded. Again, they were all quiet.

"So, what's happening in your life, Tyler?" Renee asked. "It's so very long since we saw you. Davey has missed you."

"I know what Tyler has been doing! I follow his page," Davey said. "He dated a model! Pretty girl, Tyler. I think, though, Sarah is prettier. But I saw the pictures of you."

"She's very nice," Tyler said. "She's—in Romania now. Shooting a catalog, or something like that."

"You must miss her," Davey said.

"We were casual friends."

"BFFs. That's friends with benefits," Davey told his mother, certain she wouldn't know.

"Davey!" Renee said. "Please, Tyler came as a favor. Let his private life be private."

Davey had lowered his head. He was chewing on a thumbnail, something he did, if Tyler recalled rightly, when he was nervous—or hiding something.

"You've got to be able to help somehow," Sarah said, as if she hadn't heard any of their exchange. "I'm so frustrated. I feel so worthless. And I feel terrible that I didn't keep up with her. I mean…we were friends once. I don't know what that night did to her. We all dealt with it differently. But…" She paused, inhaling a deep breath. "Sean suggested there was something—"

She broke off again. He knew what she was going to say. In the confusion with police and parents—and the horror that seemed almost worse when it was over and the garish lights were on—both Sean and Hannah had suggested there was something weird about Davey.

That it was downright scary, the way he had known something was really wrong.

"We talked. Davey told me. I think the police understood, but others didn't. My uncle taught Davey to watch people—to have excellent situational awareness, like an operative or a cop. Because people can be so cruel and mean. My uncle wanted Davey to be able to protect himself from that. Davey knew when kids wanted to—to make fun of him. He was good at avoiding such people. He was amazing at looking out for bullies. He saw that man…Archibald Lemming. He'd noticed him earlier. And he'd seen him go into that particular haunted house, and that was how he knew. But…"

"I told them," Davey said, nodding grimly. He brightened. "But they lived!"

"You were a hero," Sarah assured him.

Davey's smile faded and he looked grim. "But now Hannah is dead. And I'm afraid."

"You don't need to be afraid, Davey," Sarah assured him quickly. "You'll never be without one of us."

"Or my girlfriend!" he said brightly. "Megan," he reminded Tyler.

"Trust me, young man. Megan's mom and I will make sure you two aren't in any danger. Someone will be with you," Renee said.

"Can we still kiss and all?" Davey asked.

"We'll look away," Renee promised. She shook her head. "We're trying to keep it real—they have ten-year-old minds in grown-up bodies."

Davey giggled. Then again he looked grim. "It's scary. Sarah has to be with somebody, too."

Sarah smiled and reached over and patted his hand. "Davey, I won't be out late at night. I won't be anywhere without friends."

"You live alone."

"You could come stay here," Renee said.

"Aunt Renee," Sarah said, "I need to be near the universities. And here's the thing. We know Archibald Lemming is dead. What happened to Hannah is tragic, and one of those horrible events in life that happen to mirror another. I'll be careful. But I'm always careful. I grew up as a New Yorker, remember? I've been savvy and wary a long, long time. Besides..." She paused and looked over at Tyler. "This must be... random. The act of some horrible, twisted thing that parades as a human being. Tyler...Tyler went to war. He knows very bad things happen."

"We followed you when you were deeped," Davey said.

"Deployed," Aunt Renee said.

"We were afraid you wouldn't come back," Davey said.

"Well, I am here, and I will find out what I can to help see that this man who killed Hannah meets a justice of his own, I promise," Tyler said.

He rose. He did need to get checked into his hotel room. And he needed to find out if the people he knew had been able to pull any strings for him.

"You have my number?" Sarah asked him.

He smiled at her curiously. Of course he did. They had been texting.

"Same number, right?"

She shook her head. "Well, it's the same as about five years ago?"

Tyler frowned. "But...you have my number?"

"Has it changed?"

"Never. It's the same one I've been texting you on."

"I—I didn't get a text. Davey told me you were coming."

Davey was up on his feet and running out of the room.

"Get back here!" Sarah commanded.

Davey hadn't quite made the door. He stopped and turned around.

He looked at Sarah.

"He needed to come. Tyler needed to come. I…"

"You pretended to be me," Sarah said. "Davey! You must never do things like that!" she added with dismay.

"Davey, I should cut your texting time with Megan!" Renee said firmly.

Davey sat down, crossing his arms over his chest, his lips set stubbornly. "Tyler is here. He needed to be here." Then he threw his arms out dramatically. "Do what you will!"

"Just don't do it again! Ever!" Sarah said, horrified.

She looked at Tyler. "I'm so sorry. I never would have twisted your arm, made you come here. I mean, it was on national news, you'd hear about it, but…"

"I need to be here," Tyler said softly. "Davey is right. I've got some things to do. I'll be back with you later. We may need help from your friend."

"Kieran," she said. "Kieran Finnegan. And she's living with a man named Craig Frasier. He's—he's great. I don't know if the FBI will be investigating this, but…"

"We'll talk to him."

He wanted to hold her. To pull her to him. But she was already trying to back away. She hadn't done it—hadn't contacted him. Davey had. And Tyler needed to remember that.

"I'll be in touch later tonight," he said.

He didn't hug her goodbye. But as he went to the door, Davey raced to him. "I'm sorry, Tyler. I'm so sorry."

"It's okay, buddy, it's okay. You're right. I need to be here. The police might already have a lead on this madman, okay? But I'll be here."

He nodded to Renee and Sarah, then headed out of the house. He imagined Sarah might follow him, tell him that the years had been wasted for her, too, that she knew, just seeing him again, that…

Didn't happen.

He drove into the city and checked himself—and his car, which was as expensive to park as booking another room!—into his hotel. He had barely reached his suite before his phone rang.

And this time, it was actually Sarah.

"Tyler," she said excitedly. "We're in!"

"What?"

"This makes me feel worse than ever, but…I just got a call from a lawyer. Tyler, Hannah left a will. She has me listed as next of kin. She didn't have much money—barely enough for her funeral," Sarah said softly. "But that means that I can hire you, that it can all be legitimate, right?"

"I can work the case—even work it as if you've hired me. That's not the point. I have to form some relationships, step carefully, keep in with the police. We need everyone working together."

"But I am next of kin. You will stay, you will—"

"I will stay," he promised her softly.

And a moment later, he heard her whisper, "Thank you. Thank you!"

And then...

"Tyler?"

"Yes?"

"I am so sorry. I don't know why...I lost everyone. I should have been her friend. I really should have been her friend."

He didn't know what to say.

"Time doesn't change things like that. You were her friend. And...you're still my friend, Sarah. I still love you. I will see this through, I promise."

And he hung up before she could say anything else.

Chapter Two

"Survivor's guilt," Kieran Finnegan said softly.

Kieran was a good friend. While the hectic pace of her life—she worked as a psychologist for a pair of psychiatrists who worked frequently with the police, FBI and other law enforcement agencies, *and* helped out at the family pub—often kept her in a whirlwind where she didn't see much of her friends, she was the kind of person who was always there when she was needed.

Sarah had called her that morning.

It was Sunday noon. Hannah's body had been discovered the morning before; last night, Tyler had come to Aunt Renee's house.

And while Finnegan's on Broadway was doing a sound weekend business—they had a traditional roast entrée every Sunday that was very popular—Kieran was sitting down with Sarah. Of course, Finnegan's was in good shape that day as far as staff went, and since Sarah had once worked there, she could probably hop back in to help at any time herself, just as Kieran would do if the need arose.

Kieran had assured Sarah she would be there to spend some time with her, talk to her. As a very good friend would do.

That made Sarah feel all the worse about the lousy friend she had been herself.

"Survivor's guilt?" she repeated, shaking her head. "Honestly, I don't think so. I mean, what happened years ago…all of us survived. We survived because of Davey, though, honestly…some of the guff he had to take afterward! People wanted to know what kind of a medium or seer he was. 'Down Syndrome Boy Sees Evil.'" She was quiet for a minute. "Well, I have to admit, I was young and easily irritated, and Hannah…" She bit her lip and shrugged. "I was annoyed. She liked to have Davey around for the publicity, but then wanted me to leave him home if we were going out for the night or clubbing. She would use him when it seemed he was drawing a lot of attention, and then be irritated if we were spending any real time with him. But now…"

"From what I've gleaned through the media, her murder was brutal," Kieran murmured. "And far too similar to the method of the massacre at the theme park. Here's the thing. You're experiencing terrible guilt because Hannah is dead, and she was your friend—even it was a while ago. You both survived something horribly traumatic. But now she is dead. And you are alive. And all that happened before is rushing back. But, Sarah, you're not guilty of anything. Hannah survived that night—along with your other friends—because of Davey. You felt protective of Davey. That was only right. So quit feeling guilty. Hannah did choose to live a dangerous lifestyle. That doesn't mean what was done to her isn't every bit as horrid and criminal. But she may have put herself in danger. You have done nothing wrong. Of course, you could learn to be a bit more open to the possibility there are good people out there, and good things just might happen—and most of your friends truly love Davey."

Sarah leaned back and picked up her coffee cup, grinning. "Do I have a really big chip on my shoulder? I'm not sure whether I should enter therapy or say ten Hail Marys!"

"Do both!" Kieran suggested with a shrug. She let out a sigh. "Sarah, if you weren't really upset, you wouldn't be human, and I'd have to worry about you. Or rather, you would be a sociopath and I would have to worry about you." She shook her head. "Craig was saying that it was uncanny—the remarkable resemblance to what happened before." She hesitated. "In the actual killing, that is. Archibald Lemming found himself an amazing venue in which to carry out his bloodlust—what better than a haunted house? But it isn't him."

"It could be someone who studied him or knew him."

"Possibly."

"And someone like that doesn't stop, right?" Sarah asked.

"No," Kieran admitted unhappily. "When such a killer isn't caught and the killing stops, it's usually because he's moved on, been incarcerated for another crime or he died. This kind of thing..."

"It's not just someone who wanted Hannah dead?"

"I doubt it. What was done was overkill. Now, overkill can mean just the opposite. You see it with victims who are stabbed or bludgeoned over and over again—their killer was furious with them. Or sometimes, with someone else—and the victim they choose is the substitute for the one they want to kill. But again, remember I'm going from what was in the news. The way that this was done..."

"You think there will be more victims."

Kieran was thoughtful. "Yes—if we're talking a copycat killer who had a fan obsession with Archibald Lemming. I am afraid there will be more victims. Then again, people are clever. Maybe someone had it out for Hannah and wanted her dead specifically. Make it appear there is a psychopath or sociopath on the loose. There have been cases where several people were murdered in order to throw off suspicion when just one was the real target."

"Archibald Lemming was a psychopath, right?"

"Yes, the term applies to someone who is incapable of feeling empathy for another human being. They can be exceptionally charming and fool everyone around them—Ted Bundy, for instance. There are, however, psychopaths who turn their inclinations in a different direction—they become highly successful CEOs or hard-core business executives.

They will never feel guilt. A sociopath, on the other hand, reaches his or her state of being through social factors—neglectful parents, bullying, abuse. Some function. They can be very violent, can show extreme bitterness or hatred along with that violence, but they're also capable of feeling guilt and even forming deep attachments to others."

Sarah nodded, listening to Kieran. It was good, she figured, to have a concept of what they might be dealing with.

But dead was dead. Hannah was gone. And it didn't matter if she'd been viciously murdered by one kind of killer or another. It had been brutal.

Kieran smiled at her grimly. "I know what you're thinking. But when hunting a killer, it's helpful to have a concept of what you're looking for in his or her behavior."

"Of course! And thank you!" Sarah said quickly.

"So...Tyler Grant has come back to help?" Kieran asked. "And you were listed as Hannah's next of kin. That's good. It will allow him a lot of leeway."

"The FBI hasn't been asked in yet, right?"

"No, but Craig has a lot of friends with the police."

Kieran was referring to Special Agent Craig Frasier, FBI. They were living together—sometimes at Craig's and sometimes at Kieran's. He had the better space in NYC, so Kieran would eventually give up her apartment, most probably, and move in with him. They were a definite duo; Sarah was sure marriage was somewhere in the future for them, especially since Kieran's brothers—Declan, Kevin and Danny—seemed to accept him already as part of the family.

"Do you think…" Sarah began.

"Yes, I think!" Kieran said, smiling. She inclined her head toward the door. Tyler must have arrived. Sarah found herself inhaling sharply, her muscles tightening and her heart beating erratically.

Why? She wanted him here; she wanted…a solution. Hannah's killer caught and put away for life. She wanted…forgiveness.

Maybe it just seemed that their lives—so easy a decade ago—had come to an abrupt break. It had become a breach, and she wasn't sure things could ever be really right for her if she didn't come to terms with that.

Once upon a time, she had been so in love with him. High school! They'd been so wide-eyed and innocent, and the world had stretched before them, a field of gold.

Kieran stood, waving to him.

"You've met Tyler?" Sarah was surprised. She hadn't known Kieran in high school.

"No," her friend said, shaking her head. "He called about meeting up with Craig. I looked him up after—found some pictures online. Rock solid, so it seems."

Rock solid.

Yes, that had always been Tyler.

"But how…?"

Kieran laughed. "How do you think?"

"Davey!" Sarah said. She wasn't sure whether to be exasperated or proud of her cousin. Devious!

No, being devious wasn't really in his nature. Pretty darned clever, though!

Tyler reached the table. Sarah stood, as Kieran had. It was still awkward to see him. He'd grown into a truly striking man with his quarterback's shoulders and lean, hard-muscled physique. There were fleeting seconds when they were near one another that she felt they were complete strangers. Then there were moments when she remembered laughing with him, lying with him, dreaming with him, and she longed to just reach out and touch him, as if she could touch all that had been lost.

He was obviously feeling awkward, too. "Sarah," he said huskily, taking a second to lightly grip her elbow and bend to kiss her cheek—as any friend might do.

That touch…so faraway and yet so familiar!

"Hey, I hear Davey has been at it again," Sarah said. "This is Kieran, of course."

"Of course," Tyler said, shaking her hand.

"Craig should be here any minute. He had to drop by the office," Kieran told him.

"Thanks," Tyler said.

"Coffee? Tea? Something to eat?" Kieran asked. "We are a pub. Our roast is under way."

"I'm sure it's wonderful," Tyler told her, smiling. "I've heard great things about this place—you're listed in all kinds of guidebooks."

"Nice to know."

"I would love coffee."

"I'll see to it. Black?"

"Yep. It's the easiest," he told her.

Kieran smiled pleasantly and went to get a cup of coffee for him.

Tyler looked at Sarah.

"Craig is great. You're going to like him a lot," Sarah said. "I can't believe Davey is making all these connections."

"The kind we should have made ourselves."

Kieran was already heading back with coffee. And she was indicating the old glass-inset, wood-paneled doors to the pub.

Craig had arrived.

He hurried to the high-top table where they'd been sitting. "Hey, kid," he said to Sarah, giving her a quick kiss on the cheek. He looked at Tyler. "Tyler, right? Grant?"

"Tyler Grant. And thank you, Special Agent Frasier."

"Just Craig, please. And sorry," he added, watching Kieran arrive with coffee, "you're going to have to slurp that down. We need to get going. The man on this particular case is a Detective Bob Green. He's a twelve-year homicide vet—he worked the Archibald Lemming case years ago. You might know him when you see him, though he wasn't the one doing the interviews back then, his partner was. He's senior man on his team now. Good guy. We can join him for the autopsy."

"That's great! Thank you," Tyler told him. "I know you have other cases."

"This caught up with me in the midst of a pile of paperwork," Craig told him. "My partner is handling it for me, and my director knows where I am, so it's all good."

"What about the site where Hannah was left?"

"I can take you there." Craig turned to Kieran, slipping an arm around her. "Save us supper, huh?"

"You bet."

The affection between them wasn't anything overt or in-your-face. It was just that even the way they looked at one another seemed to be intimate.

"Okay, we're on it," Craig said. He turned and headed toward the door. Tyler looked back and nodded a thanks to Kieran. He glanced at Sarah and gave her something of an encouraging smile.

She remembered his words from last night. He would stay on this.

He loved her still.

Friends…

Yes, sometimes friends loved each other forever. Even if they couldn't be together.

Autopsy rooms could be strange places. It was where doctors and scientists studied the dead and did their best to learn from them. The NYC morgue downtown was huge; the body count was almost always high. It wasn't that so many people were murdered; New York had had less than a hundred homicides in the past year—a large number, yes, but considering that it was home to eight million-plus people, and double that number came through almost on a daily basis, it wasn't such a massive amount.

But the homeless who died so sadly in the street

came to the morgue, as did anyone who died at home or in hotel rooms, or anywhere else about the city other than with a doctor or in a hospital or directly under a doctor's care and with a known mortal disease.

Autopsy was no small neat room with refrigerated cubicles. Those existed, but for the most part, the place was a zoo comprised of the living and the dead—doctors, techs, photographers, cops, receptionists, computer crews and so on.

The living went about living—joking, taking lunch breaks, grabbing time to make appointments for themselves, call the cable company or check on the kids.

Detective Bob Green was a man in his late forties or early fifties with a thatch of neatly cut blond hair that was beginning to veer toward white, a slender face and dark almond eyes that contrasted with his pale skin and light hair. "Special Agent Frasier!" he said, greeting Craig.

Then he turned to Tyler.

He had a grave smile and a sturdy handshake. "I remember you," he told him. "I remember you all from the night at the horror park. Do you remember me?"

"Yes, I do. You were with an older detective, Mark Holiday. And a police photographer—I think his name was…Morrison. You were great with us back then, so thank you. It was hard. At first, I remembered little from that night except for the carnage and worrying about my friends," Tyler told him.

"Alex Morrison... He's still with us. So—you headed into the military and became a PI," Green said.

"I did."

"Thought you might become a cop. You were good that night. Composed. You're good in a crisis."

"Glad to hear it," Tyler told him. "Thank you."

"To be honest with you two, the autopsy already took place. But Lance—sorry, Dr. Layton—is waiting with the corpse." He paused, eyeing Tyler again. "You were there when Archibald Lemming killed all those people. We didn't know if...well, this does beat all. Of course, at this time we just have one dead woman—your friend," he added softly. "And it would be great to keep it that way. But...I was there, you were there... See what you think."

He led them into a room where a number of bodies lay on gurneys, covered properly with sheets.

A tall, thin man who reminded Tyler of Doc from *Back to the Future* stood by one of the gurneys. The ME, Dr. Lance Layton.

The man was waiting patiently for them. He greeted Craig with a smile and a polite nod. And Tyler realized he was curious about him, watching to see how he was handling being in a room with corpses. The doctor didn't extend a hand; he wore gloves, Tyler saw.

"You've seen your share of the dead, I take it?" Layton said.

"Four deployments in the Middle East, sir. Yes, I've seen my share."

Layton nodded and pulled back the sheet.

And what he saw was Hannah. What remained. She'd been such a pretty girl, olive-complexioned and with a bit of a slant to her dark eyes. She'd grown up to be an attractive woman—or she would have been, in life. If she had been alive, her eyes might have narrowed and hardened; she might have looked at the world differently. She hadn't always been the kindest or most sympathetic human being, but she'd never deliberately caused pain. She loved partying; she loved a good time. Beaches and margaritas. She'd gone toward the "dark" side—though she might have been nothing but light, had life not touched her so cruelly.

But not as cruelly as death had.

Her head sat apart from her torso and limbs. They were in different stages of decomposition.

"How was it done?" Tyler asked, and his voice was, to his own ears, thick.

"A knife. I believe she was lucky. Her killer hit the artery first. She would have bled out quickly while he continued—sawing at her."

Beheading a human being—with a knife—wasn't an easy thing to do. Strong executioners with a honed blade still had to use formidable strength; English axmen had been famous for botching the job. With a knife...

And this was Hannah.

Tyler remembered the last time he had seen her, not long after the night at the horror attraction. They hadn't talked about it the way they might have. The pictures of the dead in the "dining room" had been all too fresh in their heads. She had been quiet and grim, as they all had been, with the police. Each had been asked to give an account of what had happened. They'd been kids, ushered in and out, with protective parents or stepparents with them. A silver lining, one of the detectives had said, was that Archibald Lemming was dead. There wouldn't be a trial; they wouldn't have to stand witness.

And God help them all—they didn't need another Archibald Lemming on the streets.

Now, here, looking at the body of a young woman who had been an old friend, he found his memories were vivid and they were rushing back.

Archibald Lemming had decapitated four young people; the bodies had been seated around the table.

The heads had been upon it.

Tyler looked up at the ME and asked, "Drugs, alcohol? Anything on her, anything that would help explain how she was taken?"

Layton glanced at Detective Green. Tyler figured that Layton's loyalty was to the cop first; he'd obviously worked with Craig Frasier before. Layton wasn't telling him anything until he knew Green approved his sharing of details.

"Alcohol. And, yes, cocaine. At the rate she was imbibing…I'm not sure she'd have been long for this world as it was. She had been partying, I take it. She was last seen at a bar in Times Square," the ME told him. He glanced at Green again, and Tyler realized he must have learned that through the detective.

"It doesn't look like she put up much of a fight, but

then again, the state of the body… Being in the water can wash away a host of evidence," Layton continued. "Thankfully, she wasn't in long. Her, uh, body pieces were found at several locations along the river, but we believe they were disposed of at the same site. The current washed her up…the parts…just a bit differently. Since they were separate locations, they were discovered by different people."

"The body was cut up," Tyler noted.

"Yes, but most of the cuts are postmortem. If there is any salvation in this, I think she bled out quickly. The torture inflicted on her after…I don't think she felt. I wish I could say all this with certainty. That's just my educated opinion."

Once again, Tyler remembered the bodies around the table. They had been posed. This could be the same handiwork, as far as the beheadings went. But Hannah hadn't been posed; she'd been thrown in the river.

"It might be a copycat, it might not be," Craig murmured, obviously thinking along the same lines.

"We'll release the body toward the end of the week," Dr. Layton said. "We're holding on just in case…"

Just in case another body or body parts wash up on the riverbank again.

Detective Green, Craig and Tyler thanked him and they left the morgue.

When they were out on the street, Green looked at Tyler curiously again. "Where are you going from here?"

"Site inspections," Craig said.

"We're going to the bar where she was last seen, called Time and Time Again," Tyler said. "Then we're going along the Hudson—where the parts washed up."

"I don't think the discovery sites will help you," Green said. "Not even the killer could have known just where she'd pop up—or if she'd be taken in by a fisherman or a pleasure cruiser or what. Maybe you'll get something I didn't get at the bar. Good luck with that."

"If we find anything, we'll call immediately," Craig assured him.

Green nodded. "I know you will. Good day, my friends."

He headed off in one direction. Craig and Tyler turned in the other.

"Time and Time Again?" Craig asked.

Tyler nodded.

Time and Time Again. How tragically apropos.

Kieran didn't want Sarah going home. "You shouldn't be alone right now," she told her. "I mean, not with what has happened."

Her words surprised Sarah. She hadn't thought about being in danger herself. "I'm not being judgmental—trust me, not in any way!—but I've never led a lifestyle like Hannah was living. I mean...she was trolling for tricks. She was stripping—and not in a fine gentlemen's club. Not that a fine gentleman can't be a psychopath, right?"

"Charming, well-dressed and handsome to boot," Kieran assured her. "But the murder was so horrible... people are scared. And not just hookers. And if you're not scared, I think you should be. Anyway, wait until the guys get back, at the least. I've talked to Chef. He's saving us all a nice dinner. Until then..."

"I need to be doing something," Sarah said. "I can't just—sit here."

"What do you want to do?"

Sarah hesitated. "Look up what I can find on the past. Find out more about Archibald Lemming. Find out about the prison break. About him and his friend."

"The pub office here is all yours. We have a very nice and well-behaved computer on the desk. No one is making any entries on a Sunday. We'll be busy. Make yourself comfortable."

"Kieran, that's Declan's computer," she said uncomfortably. She knew the Finnegans, and she knew the pub. She had been grateful for such a great place to work when she had been in school.

Declan was the oldest of the Finnegan clan. He had taken on the responsibility of the pub. The others all pitched in, but Kieran's brother Danny was a tour guide and her other brother, Kevin, was an actor. The workload fell to Declan.

Kieran grabbed her hand. Declan, a handsome hunk of a man with broad shoulders, a quick smile and dark red hair, assured her that she was more than welcome to the computer, to his office and the run of the pub if need be.

Sarah found herself led down the hall to the office; Kieran signed on to the computer there.

"Knock yourself out," she told her cheerfully once Sarah was set. "I'll be wherever for the moment. When Craig and Tyler get back, you can tie up, we'll have roast and we'll see you locked in for the night."

Sarah frowned; she didn't want to be afraid. She was a New Yorker! She had never feared the subway, though she did carry pepper spray. If she'd been afraid of every perceived threat, she'd never have made it in the city.

But Kieran was gone. And Sarah didn't know where to begin—other than to key in the name "Archibald Lemming."

His crimes—even his initial crimes—had been horrendous. He'd received the death sentence, but under pressure by right-to-life groups after his sentencing, the death penalty had been altered to "life and ninety-five years." To make sure that he never got out.

But of course, he had gotten out.

Lemming's first known victim had been a kindergarten teacher. She'd been found in her home, her head almost severed from her body. He'd managed to get his second victim's head off. It had been left on a buffet table in the dining room while she'd been seated in her favorite chair. He hadn't discriminated by sex—his third victim had been a man, a plumber, who'd been found with his fingers wrapped around a beer, his torso in a recliner in the living room, his head atop the TV.

Lemming had been interviewed by the police, since he had hired the plumber to do some work in his home. It was also discovered that he'd had a flirtation going with the first victim, who had lived in his building. He'd been let go—there had been no evidence against him. Then the body and head of his landlord had been found—set up much the same as the others. And despite his "charming" protests, he'd been connected to the crimes via DNA—he'd cut himself during the last murder, and his own blood had given him away. He'd been incarcerated, where, according to prison officials, he'd been a model prisoner. Until, with Perry Knowlton—another murderer who used a knife—he'd escaped via the infirmary.

And gone on to kill and kill again in a frenzy in the "haunted" house.

Sarah sat back and breathed for a minute.

This was crazy.

She had seen the man die. He had no children—none known, at any rate. And if he'd had any offspring, it was unlikely that they knew he was their father. He'd been a loner: no wife, no girlfriend. He'd gone to work every day on Wall Street—and he'd killed by night.

She scanned the information on the page again. He was, by pure definition, the perfect psychopath. No emotion whatsoever. No regret. He was cold and brutal. He'd even murdered the man with whom he'd escaped.

Sarah frowned and started reading again.

Yes, she'd seen Archibald Lemming die.

But…

She sat back, still staring at the screen. And to her own amazement, she thought she had a theory.

Chapter Three

Being escorted back to the office by Danny Finnegan, Tyler found himself grateful that Sarah had found such a supportive group of friends.

Just going through the pub, he'd heard people call out to Danny and to one another.

"Regulars?" he asked. "They all know each other?"

Danny, a leaner, slightly younger version of his brother Declan, shrugged and grinned. "Our folks—and theirs before them—wanted it to be a real Irish pub. Well, back in the day, men had a room, and women and families had a separate one, if they were allowed in at all. But hey, progress is a good thing, right? Yeah, we like to be an Irish American *Cheers*, and we want everyone to feel welcome."

"I do," Tyler assured him.

Danny pushed open a door in the long hallway. "Tyler and Craig are back, Sarah!"

She had been very seriously staring at the computer screen and looked up quickly, a question in her eyes.

Tyler wished he could tell her that yes, simply going to the morgue had solved the whole thing.

He prayed that eventually, and sooner rather than later, they would have answers.

It wasn't going to be easy; they had nothing to go on.

"Kieran will have roast out for you all in a few minutes. We've got you at a back booth," Danny said, and left.

Tyler dropped into a chair in front of the desk.

Sarah stared at him. "It was…horrible, wasn't it?" she whispered.

He nodded. "I can't help but remember—we all had such promise."

"But did you learn anything?"

"I'm heading to the bar where she was last seen, Time and Time Again, around eight or so. If they get some of the same clientele nightly, someone might know or remember something." He hesitated a moment. "She wasn't working at the strip club anymore— she hadn't been for about two weeks. From what I understand, it was a pretty decent place. I've heard it's easy for strippers to become involved in drugs— helps them through. But there are a number of clubs run fairly well, professionally—no touching for real, and no drugs. Anyway, Hannah was fired about a week ago. Craig and I dropped by the club after we visited the sites where she was found."

"So…wow. I feel worse and worse."

"Don't. Something happened that night ten years ago. We were incredibly lucky. Thanks to Davey, we weren't killed. But we all changed. We became introverted. And when we got over it, time had passed. This was in no way your fault—you have to know that. You couldn't have stopped what happened in Cemetery Mansion, any more than you could have saved Hannah now. You have to accept that."

"I know."

"The thing is…I do think this is random. The first suspects in a murder are always those closest to the victim. Except in a case like this. There's no one really to look at—her last boyfriend was in Chicago when it happened."

"Random…" Sarah paused and took a breath. "I know this may seem far-fetched, but I have an idea who we're looking for."

Tyler couldn't have been more surprised. "Who?"

"Perry Knowlton!"

He was still for a minute. "Perry Knowlton is dead. Archibald Lemming killed him, too. Police found the ashes in a veterinary clinic before they even caught up with Lemming."

She shook her head firmly. "They never proved it!"

"What do you mean?"

"I've been reading up on Archibald Lemming and Perry Knowlton all day. I've studied every newspaper article, every piece of video. They found a body so badly burned there were no DNA samples—maybe there might have been today, but not back then. They found his prison uniform. They found trinkets he carried. But they never proved without doubt that the bone fragments and ash they discovered were the remains of Perry Knowlton."

Tyler had read up on the killers, too.

And she was right.

Before, Knowlton hadn't been someone to consider. He hadn't made any appearances over the years and had been assumed dead. He was a killer, too. A serial killer. Like his prison buddy, Archibald Lemming, he had loved to kill with knives. He hadn't been known for decapitating his victims, but for slashing them, the kill strokes being at the jugular vein.

"Maybe," Tyler said.

"But how, and where has he been? Those are the things I've been wondering. I mean, he'd be in the system. If he'd been arrested for any crime in the past ten years, his prints would be on record. They'd have known it was him. What? Did he find a distant farm somewhere and hide out for ten years? Kieran said serial killers don't stop, unless they are dead or incarcerated somewhere." She flushed, her beautiful blue eyes wide. "I know I just write science fiction novels, but I am good at research."

"Sarah, your theory is just as sound as anything else we have at the moment, that's for sure," Tyler told her. "I—I don't know. We can look."

There was a tap at the door and Kieran stuck her head in. "Roast!" she said. "You need to keep your strength up if you're going to continue working on this thing. That means actually having a meal. Craig says you're going to the bar later. Nothing to do until then except fuel up!"

"Sounds good to me," Tyler said. He rose. Sarah still had a bit of a shell-shocked look about her. He walked around the desk and reached for her hand. "Let's eat," he said.

"Dinner," she agreed.

She stood. Her palm rested in his. He couldn't believe ten years had passed and it was still incredibly good just to hold her hand.

And then she smiled at him.

And he knew. He'd waited forever to be back with her. He sure as hell hadn't wanted it to be like this... But he had never managed to fall out of love with her. And that was why nothing else in his life had ever been more than a fleeting moment in time, sex between consenting adults, panacea to ease a pain he'd refused to admit existed.

Maybe it was true that there was one person in the world who was simply everything, one person you were meant to love for a lifetime. Still, neither of them had fallen apart; they had created good lives. Responsible lives.

So why had he left?

Because she had pushed him away. And that would never lead to a lifetime of happiness. And, of course, he was still afraid she would push him away again. But at least not in the middle of a murder investigation. Not this one.

"Thank you," she said quietly.

There was something soft in her eyes. Something that made him think of years gone by.

It hurt.

And it was good, too. Oddly good.

"You're welcome," he murmured.

They made their way back down the charmingly paneled old hallway and out to the restaurant section of the pub. As promised, Kieran had a back booth for them, out of the way of the now very busy crowd. Sunday roast was apparently extremely popular.

Although Craig was careful about what he said, Tyler learned the FBI agent had been working on an organized crime case that included bodies found as the result of a rather old-fashioned but very efficient form of retribution murder—they had their feet stuck in concrete and had been dropped in the East River. "My partner, Mike, has been doing some cleanup paperwork for me, but we still have a few arrests to make. I'll be as much help as I can."

"You've opened doors for me. I'm grateful," Tyler said. "And Sarah might have a very good idea for us to pursue."

She hiked her brows in surprise and flushed again. "I hope you're not going to think I have an overactive imagination," she said.

"We definitely think you have an overactive imagination," Kieran told her. "But that's a good thing. It pays. On this, however, what do you think?"

"Tell them," Tyler urged.

And so she did.

Neither Kieran nor her boyfriend looked at her as if she were crazy.

"That's true?" Craig asked. "I remember the case—when Archibald Lemming died here on that table leg.

Of course, the entire country talked about it. But I never studied anything on Perry Knowlton. As far as the public was concerned—as far as everyone was concerned, really—the man was dead, a victim of the man he had befriended. Now that is something I can look into for you."

"That would be great."

"Excuse me," Kieran said. "Drinks, anyone?"

They opted for iced tea all around and she disappeared to get it. Another smiling waitress arrived with their plates.

The food was really good.

The conversation became lighter. They learned that Kieran and Craig had met during a diamond heist. Because of Kieran's employers, Dr. Fuller and Dr. Miro, she was able to help Craig with a number of cases—recently one that had involved the deconsecrated old church right behind the pub. "My brother was affected by that one... He'd been in love with a victim," Kieran said softly. "That's Kevin. You haven't met him yet, Tyler. But I'm sure you will!"

Tyler told them he was living on Beacon Hill. He described his daily work. "I take on a lot of missing-children cases," he said. "When I'm lucky, I find them—most often, they're runaways. When they're not...I have a great relationship with the Boston PD, which is very important. I won't work possible-cheating-spouse cases—too sordid. I have worked murder cases—a number of cold cases. It wasn't always that way, of course, but working the cheating spouse thing just seems nasty—and finding justice for someone feels really good."

"Have you ever considered coming back to New York, Tyler?" Kieran asked.

"It's home. One never knows," he said.

"Boston, New York…so many great cities!" she said. And then she looked at her watch. "Whoa. Well, dinner with you two was great. I wish we were heading to a play or a movie now, but I know you want to stay focused. It's eight o'clock."

"Time to go," Tyler said, rising.

"Are you going with him?" Kieran asked Craig.

"I have to head to the office for at least an hour or so," he replied. "Hey, this man is a good investigator. He'll do fine."

Sarah had risen, as well. "I'm going with you," she said.

"Sarah," Tyler protested. "That's not a great idea."

"I can help."

"How?"

"I can make you look human and sweet—better than looking like a linebacker out to tackle someone!"

TIME AND TIME AGAIN was off Forty-Second Street and the Times Square area, but far enough away from the theater district on Ninth Avenue to just miss most of the theater-going crowd.

It would best be described, Sarah thought, as a *nice* dive bar.

She definitely wanted all her facilities about her,

but deeply disappointed the bartender by ordering a soda with lime.

"Don't you want a Ninth Avenue Special, a Dive-Bar Exotic or a Yes, It's Time Again?" he asked her.

He was a young man of maybe twenty-five. Cheerful and flirty.

Sarah was sitting at the bar; Tyler was meeting with the night manager in his office.

"No, thanks. Just the soda water."

"Your friend a cop?" he asked her.

She shook her head, smiling though, and looked around. The place was decorated with old posters that depicted the city during different eras. They helped cover the fact that the bar really needed to be painted.

"No, Tyler isn't a cop."

"But he's in there asking about that girl," the bartender said. He had a neatly trimmed beard and mustache combo, and she wondered if he was a student at one of the city's colleges.

"Yes, he's asking about Hannah Levine," she told him softly.

"I'm Luke," he said, looking down the bar to see if he was needed. He wasn't. He leaned on it. "The cops have already been all over us. She was carrying one of our promo matchboxes—that's how they knew she'd been here." He grimaced. "They have raised lettering—really swank matches for this place, but we get a mixed clientele. We cater to the local music scene."

"Nice," she replied. He was friendly, and she decided she might be able to help the investigation. She could ask questions, too, and maybe in a different way. "Are you from New York?"

"Nope. Akron, Ohio. Loving being here. Don't be deceived by appearances. This is actually a great place. Yes, we have a few lowlifes hanging around. But it's honest work for me and helps pay the bills."

"Hannah was my friend," she said softly.

"Oh?" He seemed surprised. He leaned closer to her. "You don't look like a junkie."

"Hannah wasn't on heroin," she said defensively.

"No, just everything else. She came in here frequently. The owner had barred her for a while, but... people liked her. She just—well, she looked for tricks here, you know."

Sarah winced.

"Hey, I'm so sorry. I guess you hadn't seen her in a while."

"No, I hadn't. But..."

"I can see you care." He straightened and said, "Excuse me," and hurried down the length of the bar, speaking to customers seated on stools along the way. He refilled a few drinks, whispered to someone and then headed back to speak with Sarah.

"I don't know what it was with her!" Luke said. He lowered his voice. "We dated a few times, but then...I found out she was hooking. I...well, that didn't work for me. I want to have a wife I'll grow old with, kids. Hannah said she'd never settle down. But we didn't part badly. We were friends. I tried to help out, give her food—pay her bar tab when she walked out. She was her own worst enemy. Sometimes I thought she was committing slow suicide. Even when she had people trying to help her, she'd laugh them off. She said she loved the danger of hooking, you know?"

Sarah did know. Hannah had wanted to be on the edge—she'd wanted to skydive, ride the fastest coaster, speed on the FDR.

"I don't care what she was doing. What happened shouldn't have happened to her or to anyone!" Sarah said passionately.

"No! Of course not! I didn't mean that. Just that…I don't know who she might have met, who could have done such a terrible thing…"

His voice trailed off as he realized he obviously didn't need to remind Sarah what had happened.

"Were you working when she was here?" Sarah asked him.

"I was coming for the late shift. But I was just outside. Coming in."

"And you talked to her?"

He nodded. Sarah thought she saw the glint of tears in his eyes and his voice was husky when he said, "She gave me a big hug and a kiss on the cheek and told me she 'was about to go roll in some dough.' I assumed that meant she had met up with a rich guy willing to pay a nice price. She was so pretty. Even… even with the drugs and alcohol. And nice. No matter what, she had something about her. A core that had some real warmth, you know?"

"I do know," Sarah assured him. She cleared her throat. "Did you tell the police what she said?"

"I wasn't interviewed. I wasn't actually in the bar

when she was here, so the manager never called me to talk to the police."

"And you didn't volunteer to help?" Sarah asked.

"Hey. They were trying to paint a picture of her I don't agree with—that she was a druggie whore who got what was coming to her."

"That can't be true. Any sensible, decent person knows that, whatever someone's lifestyle, they don't deserve such a horror 'coming to them.' That can't be—"

She was suddenly interrupted by Tyler's deep voice right behind her. "Whatever made you think the world was filled with sensible and decent people?"

She fell silent. The bartender was looking at Tyler. Sarah quickly introduced the two. They shook hands as Tyler crawled up on the stool next to Sarah's.

"You're not a cop?" Luke asked him warily.

Tyler shook his head. "I'm a PI, in from Boston. Mainly here because, as I'm sure Sarah told you, Hannah was a friend."

"Pity you guys weren't around when she was still living," he murmured.

"Yes, we're well aware of that," Sarah said.

"Hey," Tyler said. The word wasn't spoken angrily, nor was it shouted. But it was filled with the fact that Sarah could not be blamed—nor could any of them.

"A sick killer is responsible, no one else. When she was a kid, no one could tell Hannah what to do. I sincerely doubt she'd have listened now. But we were her friends," Tyler went on. "And we will see that justice is done for her."

"Okay, okay!" Luke said, hands in the air. "Look,

I'm sorry I didn't go bursting into the office and say hey, yeah, I knew Hannah. I don't know who killed her..."

His voice faltered suddenly.

"What is it?" Sarah asked.

"A man."

"A man?" Tyler asked.

Luke nodded. "He was in here several times a couple of weeks ago. I thought that he was watching Hannah. No way out of it, with those cat eyes of hers... bedroom eyes, you know what I mean? Anyway, he was watching her."

"Was he...old, young? Can you describe him?" Tyler asked.

"Well, he was average. He wore a low-brimmed hat all the time—I sure don't know his eye color or anything like that. Narrow face. Wore a coat, too. But then, you know, when it's cold, people don't always take their coats off in bars. Especially this one—the heating system isn't so great."

"Anyone else unusual?" Tyler asked him.

"I'll think...honestly, I'll think about it. But as far as this place goes... I mean, describe unusual. We get all kinds. Some hardworking, partying-on-Friday-nights kind of people. Drug dealers now and then. But Willie—you met Willie, the night manager, right?" he asked, looking at Tyler. "You were just in talking with him, right?"

Tyler nodded.

"He doesn't like drug dealers or junkies. He can

usually ferret them out and he's as tall and muscle-bound as you are, dude," he said, glancing quickly at Tyler and then grimacing at Sarah as if they shared a great joke. "I think they hired him because they don't need a bouncer when he's on. Also, he's the owner's cousin. Owner is in Utah, so... But you see, Hannah left here—after that, we don't know."

"I know," Tyler said. "And, listen, the cops on this really are good guys. If I can get them to send a sketch artist down here, do you think you could help us get some kind of an image of the guy in the hat and the coat?"

"I'll go you one better," Luke promised. "Bring your guy down. We'll also post that we need any help—no matter how minute—anyone can give. How's that?" He pointed across the room to a large bulletin board. "Trust me. People will want to help. Kind of like back in the days of Jack the Ripper, you know? People may like to think this guy only went after a prostitute and he won't target them. But this kind of thing..." A shudder shook his whole body. "This is terrifying!"

"Hey, is there actually a bartender in here?" someone shouted from the end of the bar.

"Hang on, there, Hardy! Give your liver a breather! I'm on the way!" Luke said. He nodded to the two of them.

"Did you pay yet?" Tyler asked Sarah.

"No." She scrambled in her tote bag for her wallet, but Tyler had already set a bill on the bar.

"I think I'm supposed to be paying you," she said. "For your services."

He stared at her and smiled slowly. "I was that good, huh?"

She realized just how her words might be taken, and yet of course he was teasing.

Still…

Ten years between them.

She felt the blood rise to her cheeks. She had not blushed this much since…well, since forever.

"I meant I'm next of kin, or so Hannah said. I'm hiring you to find her killer."

He shook his head. "I'm going to find this killer for Hannah. And for all of us," he said.

TYLER HAD BARELY gotten into his hotel room after dropping Sarah off at her place when his phone rang.

"Tyler?"

He was curious the caller had voiced the question, as he always answered his phone with one word, his surname, "Grant."

But despite time and distance, he knew the caller.

"Sean," he said.

"Yeah, it's Sean. Hey, how are you? I know this is out of the blue, but…"

There was fear in Sean's slightly garbled and wandering words.

"I'm here. In New York."

"Because of Hannah?"

"Yes."

"Thank God!" Sean said. "I mean, you were in the military, right? You, uh, know your way around a gun and all that."

"I know my way around a gun and all that," he agreed.

"I'm afraid they're after us," Sean said.

Tyler hesitated. Then asked, "Sean, who are *they*? Everyone thinks what happened to Hannah is horrendous, but why would any 'they' be after all of us?"

"You don't know the latest. Oh, well, it just broke. Maybe you haven't heard."

As Sean spoke, Tyler realized he had another call coming in—from Craig Frasier.

"Excuse me. I'll be right back with you," he told Sean. "Craig?"

"There's been another murder. Body and head left in a park by the FDR. There was ID. Her name was Suzie Cornwall."

Suzie?

Sarah's best friend? God, no.

"Bob Green called me. You can join us at the park. I'll text the address."

He switched the call back over. "Sean, my God, I'm so sorry—"

"Oh, Suzie—our Suzie—is here with me."

"What? Listen, Sean—"

"No, no, I heard on the news. Suzette Cornwall was murdered. But it's not our Suzie. Our Suzie is here, with me. We're married now, you probably know, so she's Suzie Avery. The cops found me—I guess as a Suzie Cornwall's husband, in whatever database. She was Suzie Cornwall, too. But…oh, Lord! Our Suzie is here. She's fine. But that's just it, don't you see? He—or they!—got Hannah. They're looking for us, Tyler. They're looking for us—the group at Cemetery Mansion that year."

That was crazy. Just crazy. The only person who might want some kind of revenge was Archibald Lemming. And Lemming was dead. Tyler had seen the table leg protrude right through his body.

He'd seen the blood. The ripped and torn flesh, down to the organs and bone. Lemming was not alive. And Tyler had lived with the fact that he was at least partially responsible for that man's death…no matter if he was a murderer the world was better off without.

Perry Knowlton? Was he really out there? Had Archibald Lemming helped him pretend to die—so that he could live?

"Tyler? Help!" Sean said softly.

"All right, listen, Sean. You and Suzie stay close and keep your doors locked. Don't go out tonight. Stay in until I know what's going on. You hear me?"

"I hear you. Loud and clear. Door is locked. But please, don't you see? He killed Hannah Levine. Now he's killed a Suzette Cornwall. We're all supposed to die, Tyler. I don't know why, except that we were there. We were there."

"I'll be in touch. Just stay put. Where are you living now?"

"Brooklyn. Got a little house."

It was too bad Sean wasn't living in a tiny apartment with no windows and one door.

"Windows—check all the windows. Make sure you're secure."

"Got it. You'll call me?"

"As soon as possible. I'm meeting the cops at the site."

He hung up; he didn't have time to waste on the phone. He put a call through to Sarah. Her phone rang a few times, and in those split seconds he felt debilitating panic setting in.

Then she answered.

"Sarah, listen to me. I'm asking Detective Green to get a man out to your aunt's house. Now I do think we're all in danger."

"What? What are you talking about?"

"Have you seen the news?"

"No."

"Okay, it's not the Suzie who was our friend, but a Suzie Cornwall was murdered. I just talked to Sean. They're fine. But I'm going to stop by for you. I need to get you somewhere safe. You can stay at Kieran's with her for now. Craig has been living there, mostly, I guess, so I am assuming it's pretty darned safe. You have to lock yourself in..."

"A woman named Suzie Cornwall was murdered?" she asked.

"Not our Suzie."

"Poor woman. Oh, my God, poor woman!"

"Sarah, listen to me. Don't open your door until you hear my voice!"

"Right, right. I won't," she promised.

"And call Davey and Renee. Tell them to stay put until we figure something out."

Tyler hung up, and then, with his wits more thoroughly about him, he dialed Craig back. Craig let him know that yes, of course Kieran would be happy to have Sarah come stay with her. He should have said something; he had thought it was a given.

Tyler thanked him and headed out. His hotel wasn't far from Sarah's place on Reed Street. It seemed as if the distance had somehow become greater since the last time he drove it.

He left his car in the street, not caring what kind of a fine he might get, and took the steps to her apartment two at a time.

But Sarah was ready to go. She had a little bag with her. She looked at him with wide eyes, shaking her head. "That's too much to be a coincidence, right?"

"It's too close," he agreed.

"My theory...I think it has to be right!" she whispered.

"It may be right. Listen, I'm taking you to—"

"Kieran's. I figured. Where else could you drop me at midnight—or is it 1:00 a.m. yet?"

He just nodded.

Then he told her, "I'll find out more when I see the crime site."

They hurried out to the car and he got her in safely before he jumped back in the driver's seat. When they got to Kieran's place in SoHo, he parked the car in the street again.

"Go on—I'll run in!" Sarah told him.

"Not in this lifetime," he answered, leaving the car and taking her arm.

Kieran lived above a karaoke bar. Someone was warbling out Alice Cooper's "The Man Behind the Mask" as they made their way up.

The singer wasn't so bad. His choice of song seemed grating.

Of course, Sarah knew which unit was Kieran's door. She stopped in front of it.

Tyler reached out to knock.

And then it touched him that they were on the run from an unidentified threat, and he was on his way to go see the corpse of a woman—an innocent victim—who, just earlier today, had surely believed she had years left before her.

Life was fleeting.

He turned, pulled Sarah into his arms and kissed her. It was a hard kiss, hurried and passionate, hotly wet and very sloppy. She was surprised at first, but then she returned his kiss, and when he released her, she looked at him breathlessly, with confusion.

"Tyler—"

"I love you. I've always loved you. And so help me God, we will survive this!"

Kieran's door opened; she'd heard something. She had expected them. Tyler saw one of her brothers was there, as well.

"Danny is going to hang with us," she said.

"Great," Tyler said. "Okay—"

"Don't even say 'lock up.' I'm a New Yorker, and I live with Craig!"

He actually smiled at that. Then he turned and left. No cops had ticketed his car and no tow company had taken it away.

He drove quickly and competently.

He needed to reach the crime scene.

To see everything in situ.

He had to get there.

And, dear lord, how he dreaded getting there, as well.

Chapter Four

Danny Finnegan was really a great guy.

Once upon a time, Sarah and he had almost dated. She'd somehow known that it couldn't be a forever kind of thing between them, so they'd stayed friends.

Danny, she thought, had realized the same thing. They were never going to be friends with benefits, either—it would be just too awkward for them and the entire family. And having the Finnegan family as friends was something special; they'd tacitly known that anything between them—other than great friendship—could destroy it all.

And still she loved him as a friend, as she did Kieran.

If it weren't for the fact that two people had been murdered in a fashion reminiscent of a decade-old massacre, it might have been just a late evening with friends.

Kieran made hot chocolate and set out cookies; Danny diverted Sarah with weird stories about the city. "Believe it or not, this lady kept her son's corpse in the house for years—up in Brooklyn. She didn't kill him—poor guy died young of disease. But she kept him—and the only reason the body was discovered was that she was hospitalized herself. A relative went to get some things for her and…well, the son was down to skeletal remains. I've heard stories about other people keeping corpses, but I know this one is true! The papers all covered it. We're a great state—and so weird. Oh, not in the city, but up in Elmira, John Brown's widow—she being the widow of the John Brown's raid John Brown!—received a head. A skull, really. Another man named John Brown died down in Harpers Ferry, a skull was found and everyone said that it was John Brown's—so they sent it to her."

"Ugh. What did she do?"

"Sent it back, of course!" Danny said.

Sarah smiled, knowing he knew she'd grown up in the city and would be aware of the history of the state, but maybe not all the most bizarre bits and pieces of fact and lore.

"Hey, Cooper Union had the first elevator shaft—not elevator, actually. Otis hadn't come along yet, but when building, Cooper had the basic idea, using a round shaft!"

Sarah laughed. "I think I did hear something about that years ago—NYU students often hung out with Cooper Union people."

Her phone rang. She glanced at the number and was surprised to see that despite a few hardware upgrades over the years, Suzie Cornwall's number was still in her contacts.

She answered quickly. "Suzie?"

"Hey. You okay? I'm sorry. I shouldn't have called. I mean, it was okay—not okay, Lord! I'm sorry, it was not okay, it was terrible, horrible, when Hannah was killed. But…it didn't really terrify me. It saddened me, but it didn't terrify me. Sarah, now he's killed a *Suzie Cornwall*. Oh, my God. That poor woman. She was killed for having my name! I'm so scared, Sarah. So scared. Do you think that…Davey could help?"

Stunned, Sarah stared at the phone. "Suzie, hey, hey, yes, of course I know you're scared. But…Davey is a young man with Down syndrome. He isn't a medium, he isn't magical. That night…he saw Archibald Lemming slinking around. He saw him go into the house. My uncle taught him to be wary. How to really notice things, to watch out for people because, sad as it may be, the world is full of bullies who want to hurt those who are at a disadvantage instead of helping them. He didn't want Davey to fall victim to someone who meant him ill."

"But…he *knew* that night!" Suzie whispered. "Oh, I'm sorry. Sean said this wouldn't make any sense."

"Congratulations, by the way. I 'liked' it when I saw that you two had married, but I figured a zillion other people did, too. You looked beautiful."

"Yes, yes. Thank you. I think I actually saw your 'like.' I should have called or written then, or…you know. Oh, but I've bought all your books!"

"Thanks. I didn't think you were a sci-fi fan."

"I'm not."

"Well, then, thank you very much."

"Oh, but they were good. Oh, Sarah! I'm so scared."

"You're home, right? Tyler told you to go home and stay there and lock in, right?"

"But what do we do in the morning? Sean and I both have jobs. He works down on Wall Street. I'm up by the park at the new department store there— I'm a makeup artist. Sean is a stock broker."

"Maybe, just tomorrow, you shouldn't go in. Maybe they can arrange police protection."

"For the rest of our lives? Sarah, they have to find this maniac."

Both Kieran and Danny could hear Suzie through the phone, she was talking so loudly. Sarah looked at them both, shaking her head.

"No," she said firmly, gazing at Danny and Kieran. "Until they find the killer."

"It's Lemming. It's Archibald Lemming. He's back. He's come back, and he knows we were there. He's going to kill us all."

"It's not Archibald Lemming. We saw him die."

"He's come back—somehow."

"No. It's someone just as sick, using what happened."

"But…how? How is this person finding us?"

"He made a mistake—he didn't find you. Unless this is sheer happenstance and he killed a woman who happened to have the same name, or your maiden name."

"Lemming must be whispering from the grave. He'll keep killing, it wasn't happenstance. He's after me."

"He'll be stopped."

"But what if—"

"Tyler is back in New York," Sarah said simply. "And I know he won't stop."

THE BODY OF the woman was seated on a park bench, hands rested easily in her lap. If she just had a head, it would have appeared she had simply decided to relax a minute and enjoy the beauty of the park.

She'd been wearing a red sweater and jeans. All around the neck area, the sweater was darkened; blood had dried into it.

As Tyler arrived, Craig came forward, telling the officer who was keeping the crowd back that Tyler was with him.

"We're on it now," Craig told him, referring to the FBI. "This morning, with this second kill and the name of the victim, the police chief decided to bring us in, along with every law enforcement agency in the near vicinity. He's a good guy. No jurisdictional bull with him. He wants murders solved."

He'd spoken as they came to the body. Police photographer Alex Morrison was there, snapping pictures quickly. Detective Bob Green was present, too, leaning close to the victim, but not too close. Dr. Lance Layton had been called out; he had already arrived, as well.

Thankfully, none of them looked at Tyler as if he didn't belong, or as if he were an interloper.

"No defensive wounds," Layton said. "But the bastard did saw through her neck with a blade—a serrated blade, so it appears. Might have drugged her first. Pray that he did, the poor thing! Had to have—no one could feel that kind of pain and not react."

"The head?" Craig asked quietly.

"It was left in a kid's swing," Green said. "Doc had it moved—it's in the back of the wagon."

He was referring to Dr. Layton's vehicle. The back door to the van was open, an officer in uniform standing guard before it.

"We'll take a look," Craig said grimly.

They did; the officer knew Craig and gave way.

The head was in a sterile container.

Her hair had a brown base, but had been multicolored in blues and greens and pinks, just as many women were coloring their hair. Though it was difficult to tell from a severed head—all life and vitality gone—it appeared she had been a bit older than their Suzie. Judging from the headless body, she had probably been about the same height and weight.

"How did he get her here?" Tyler wondered aloud. The FDR was just above them. The park was surrounded by apartment buildings, all of which had storefronts at the bottom. It was a typical New York City neighborhood—the park offering some trees and fake grass, but all around it, the congestion of giant buildings and all the trappings needed to house millions of people on an island.

"She was found after dark by some folks who jumped the fence—a babysitter who'd lost her phone here. I don't think the killer thought she'd be found until morning," Craig told Tyler. "The media got hold of it just about the same time as the police, so God knows what pictures are out there. They had her name first—she lived in that building just over there. No ID on her, but our teenage babysitter knew her because they live in the same building. Her name is on the buzzer in the foyer. No night guard or desk clerk in the place. No cameras. The cops are doing a door-to-door now, but…so far, no one saw anything."

"He killed her elsewhere and got her in here fast."

Tyler looked out at the crowd watching the scene. The killer could be there—with the others, watching them all, enjoying the fruit of his labors.

"Crime scene techs are going over the place with a fine-tooth comb," Craig said. "We're hoping to hell the officers or the techs will find something—anything. And," he added grimly, "we're hoping Lance will tell us she was drugged and unconscious before this happened. Press conference first thing, autopsy right after. Until then…"

"I need to be with Sarah," Tyler said. But he paused, looking around the scene. The park, with the shaded benches for moms and dads and babysitters. The colorful playground created for children, with crawl bars, slides and multileveled platforms.

The park was fenced, but the fence was wood and easily scaled.

"Facts we have will be coming through email,"

Bob Green said, walking over to them. He always seemed to be studying Tyler. Tyler just stared back at him. He supposed he was a curiosity to the detective. He had been there when Archibald Lemming had attacked a group of teenagers in a haunted house. When there had been so much fake blood it had been hard to figure out where the real blood began. "We'll share all information on this immediately, to facilitate working together. This has to be stopped. The mayor called me personally. I have a meeting with my guys and the FBI at the crack of dawn, and we have to be ready for the press conference. We'll have the park roped off for the next week, at least." He lowered his head, letting out a sigh of disgust. "Kids. Little kids come here. The babysitter…she's a student at NYU. All of about twenty. Can you imagine a little one walking in on a sight like that?"

"No one should ever have to walk in on a sight like that," Tyler said.

"Is there…anything you can think of, anything about Lemming, anything at all that might help?" Green asked him.

"Lemming died that night. We don't believe, however, that the man with whom he escaped is dead."

Green frowned. "Ashes and bone fragments and his prison uniform were found. Lemming used Perry Knowlton to escape, then he killed him."

"He's the only man who would really know exactly how Archibald Lemming worked," Tyler said. "And there was no DNA. There sure as hell were no fingerprints. There's no proof the man is dead."

"At my office we're going to work on the concept that he might be alive," Craig said.

Green nodded slowly. "And he's out for...revenge?"

"Possibly."

"Then you're all in danger. You, Sarah, Sean Avery and the other Suzie Cornwall. And Davey Cray," he added softly.

"And Davey," Tyler agreed. "Can you give them protection?"

"I can. And you might be right. Then again, the killer could be anyone. There are sick people out there who fall even more sickly in love with criminals and killers. Especially serial killers. Some of the fan mail those guys get in prison...it's enough to make your hair stand on end. But we need something to work with. Anything."

He was still looking at Tyler, apparently wanting an answer.

"As you said, our lives are in danger. If I had any kind of an idea, I guarantee you, I'd share it."

"There's nothing, nothing from that night...?"

"I remember Archibald Lemming coming at me with a blade. I was in shock. I was terrified for myself and the others. Sick from what I saw. And then Sarah and Davey were there—and I pushed Lemming off us, and we saw Lemming die. We can't look to the past. It isn't him doing these things. But I believe it is someone who knew him."

"Let's get out of here—it's nearly three in the morning," Craig said. "We can think it all out for hours, talk it all out…but there's nothing more we can do here."

There wasn't. The dead woman's torso was being loaded for removal to the morgue; they would, at that point, just get in the way of the officers and techs working. She obviously had been killed elsewhere; she'd been displayed. Not thrown in a river. Displayed.

"Interesting," Tyler said.

"Yep."

"Yep?"

"You're wondering how, if the park was locked, one man got the body over the fence. It's damned unlikely he just waltzed in with the corpse and a head."

"And yet, could two people working together be quite so sick?"

"I guess we need sleep," Craig said. "Clear heads are better."

They had separate cars; they headed to them, both aware they were going back to Kieran's in the Village over the karaoke sushi bar.

Walking down the street, Tyler was aware of the way his Smith and Wesson sat in the holster at the back of his waistband.

Because he couldn't help but wonder if someone was watching.

This was Kieran's neighborhood, not Sarah's. Sarah lived far down south on the island, on Reed Street.

And the killer didn't know everything; after all, he'd murdered the wrong Suzie Cornwall.

Tyler wondered how many other people might have the same names in New York City. None of the group had an unusual name.

Craig had parked ahead of him. He caught up and they walked together. "You think he's had enough for one night?" he asked Tyler.

"Hannah hasn't been dead more than a week—and from what the ME said, she's probably only been dead about five days. Water hides a lot of truths. And now...I don't know. Hard to tell if he's just getting started—if he's been locked up for years, or murdering kittens and puppy dogs for practice."

"I think this person has killed in this manner before," Craig said. "He knows just how hard it is to decapitate someone with a knife. He enjoys the struggle to manage it all, and he's proud of himself for doing it."

"There's got to be something on this guy somewhere."

"Somewhere. Thing is, how do you suddenly do things so horrible? Where has this guy been? How do we have a repeat of Archibald Lemming now—out of the blue?"

"There is something, somewhere," Tyler said with determination. "We just have to find it."

They had reached the stairs to Kieran's apartment.

The karaoke club had gone quiet; it would be dawn in another few hours.

Kieran answered the door as soon as she heard Craig's voice. "Anything?" she asked anxiously.

Danny and Sarah had come to stand behind her. They all looked at Craig and Tyler expectantly.

"A corpse, as grisly as you would expect," Tyler said.

"And her name was…Suzie Cornwall?" Sarah said. "For sure?"

"From everything we understand," Craig said. "Cops are canvassing the neighborhood and the forensic team is busy," he added.

"This one was more like…before, right?" Sarah asked.

Tyler hesitated to share the gory details. "She wasn't tossed. In two pieces. She was in two pieces, but set up for shock value. No haunted house, but an audience of children and young mothers, if she hadn't been found until morning."

"We'll know more then. Kieran, I think we should talk to your fine doctors, Fuller and Miro, tomorrow," Craig said. "There will be a press conference and then we'll go to the autopsy, but after that…"

"Of course," Kieran said.

"Not that you're not brilliant and haven't learned just about everything from them," Craig told her.

"Sure, sure…no charming sweet talk, huh? I was about to pull out our blow-up beds. We all have to get some sleep, even if it's only a few hours. Danny is going to hang in and we've actually got it all covered. I figured I'd take Sarah and we'd pull a girl thing and claim the bedroom, and then one of you on the sofa and two on the floor—"

"I have a hotel room, and it's under the business

name. I don't need to make it more crowded here,"
Tyler said.

"Oh, but it's so late," Kieran protested. "Or early."

"It's okay. There's no traffic," he insisted.

"I'll go with you," Sarah said.

"What?" He said the word sharply, though he
didn't mean to be so abrupt.

It didn't matter. She ignored the tone. "I'll go with
you."

"We should have gone to Craig's place—much bigger and nicer," Kieran admitted.

"It's all right, the hotel is great. I'm on the twenti-
eth floor. There's security on at night. And I was in
the service. I wake up at just about anything," Tyler
said.

Sarah already had her bag. She was coming with
him.

"All right. Let us know you get there okay, huh?"
Kieran asked.

"Hey, this guy has hit only vulnerable women so
far. I'm not vulnerable," Tyler assured her. "But yes,
we'll text as soon as we're there."

He'd never agreed Sarah should come. Out in the
hall, once Kieran had closed and locked the door, he
turned to her. "This isn't a good idea."

"Probably not," she agreed.

"You can just stay with your friend—"

"Too crowded."

"You'd have the bedroom—"

"Look, you'll be leaving again, after all this, I
know that. I don't really know what I'm doing, either.

But this has happened. We're together now. And I...I know you. Whatever this is, for however long...I'd rather be with you right now. Kieran is great. Craig is great. Neither of them was at Cemetery Mansion."

"We need to be careful, over everything else."

"Yes, I know. But right now I want to be with you. Yes, you left me before. I expect you'll leave again. And that's all right. That's—that's the way it has to be."

He hesitated, ready to open the door to the street. He looked at her and said softly, "No, don't even try to tell me you believe it happened in that order. You left me long before I ever decided I had to go."

He didn't give her a chance to protest. He opened the door and hurried her out to the car.

He wondered if he should think it was wrong, crazy. He knew where this was going.

And he could only be grateful for the moment.

"So, WELCOME TO my temporary castle," Tyler said, opening the door to his room.

It was a slightly nicer hotel room at a middling upscale chain hotel. There was a small sitting area with a sofa Sarah assumed opened up to an extra bed, a large bath and a very inviting, big bed with some kind of an extra-squishy mattress that promised a great night's sleep.

It was barely night anymore and she wasn't really intending to sleep. Not right away.

Tyler locked the door and slid the bolt. Sarah had

wandered in and set down the small bag she had packed to head over to Kieran's.

"My favorite chain. I have one of those 'frequent stayer' cards with them."

"You're in hotels often?" Sarah asked.

"I travel around some. Business."

"But not often in New York."

"I avoid New York," he said.

"But you're here now," she said.

He turned, studying her, his hands on his hips. "And you—you're here right now."

She nodded, not sure about her next actions. She had forgotten just how she loved everything about Tyler. Even the way he stood now, curious and confident. Not aggressive—just confident. They'd both had it so easy when they'd been younger. She had known she'd gotten lucky—not just because of his easy laughter, kindness and natural charm. She was lucky because they had found each other. They'd never been the brightest, best or most beautiful; they had just fallen in together when they'd been fifteen and sixteen, when she'd dropped some papers, when they'd both reached down to gather them up and had crashed heads. And then laughed. They were new then—new kids at a new school.

She shrugged off the memory and took a hard look at the man standing before her.

"You said you still loved me."

"I do." He didn't hesitate. "And I believe you love me."

"And that sometimes, love just isn't enough."

"Right. Sometimes love just isn't enough."

"But for tonight…"

"Or today," he said drily, glancing over at the clock on the mantel.

"For now…"

She thought he was going to say something like "Come over here!" Or that he would take the few steps to reach her.

But he didn't. "For now…I really need a shower. I was…there. Anyway, a shower."

He turned away, pulling a small holster from the rear waistband of his jeans and setting it on the little table by the bed. He shed his jacket and shoes. She was still just standing there, and he shrugged and headed on into the bathroom.

He didn't close the door. She wasn't sure whether that meant she was being given an invitation or not.

Sarah quickly slid out of her sweater and jeans, glad he had gone into the shower. She wasn't sure she could have disrobed with anything like sensuality anymore—it had been too long.

Awkward! That was her theme emotion with him now. Once, everything had been so easy. And now…

Naked, she tiptoed toward the bathroom door. The shower was very large. Tyler was standing under the spray, just letting the water rush over him. She knew, of course, what he was feeling. He felt that he smelled of death and decay, and the water would never be cleansing enough. She had felt that way after the night at the Cemetery Mansion. And for a long time afterward.

She opened the shower door and slipped in behind him, encircling his waist with her arms and laying her head against his back.

He turned, pulling her to him, gently lifting her chin and her face. His mouth moved down upon hers, soft and wet and steaming. He touched gently at first, so that she barely knew if the steam and heat was him or a whisper of the water beating all around them. Then the pressure of his kiss became hard, his mouth parted hers and she felt his tongue, and with it, wings of fire crept through her memory and more.

The water sluiced over and around them, deliciously hot and sensual. His hands held her tight against him first, and when it seemed her breasts were all but welded to his chest, she felt his palms slide seductively down her back, his fingers teasing along her spine. He pressed his lips to her shoulder, and her collarbone, and then his eyes rose to hers. The way he looked at her…the past and present rolled into one. They had been so young once.

His eyes were no longer young. And yet she loved everything she saw within them, even if that wisdom meant he would leave her again, and this, this thing between them that was so unique, would be nothing but a memory.

He reached behind him to turn off the water. And he grinned suddenly. "I was thinking of some great, cinematic moments of romance. I should sweep you up, press you against the tile, make mad love to you here and now…"

"Except one of us would slip on the soap and we'd

end with broken limbs?" she asked, smiling in turn, a little breathless, surprised she'd been able to speak.

"Something like that," he said. "And we have a dreamy mattress…and, hmm, neither of us has to do the laundry. Let me try this!"

He thrust the shower door open and stepped out, and then surprised her so much she gasped before laughing as he swept her up in his arms. "There's no staircase for me to carry you up dramatically, but…"

"We're soaking!"

"The heat is on—no pun intended—and we'll dry."

And still she smiled. He walked the few steps needed and let her fall into the softness of the bed, and then he came down in turn. He was immediately by her side, half atop her, finding her lips again with his own, his hands skimming over her, touching her with caresses that made her forget everything but a longing for more. They seemed to meld into a kiss again, rolled with the pile of soft covering, and then his lips found hers, left them, moved down the length of her body, hovering here and there over her breasts, then snaking downward. He caressed her thighs with kisses and erotic finger play, and she writhed, twisting to come back around to him, to touch him, press her lips against his skin, taste the cleanliness of his naked flesh, the warmth of him, the fire, the essence…

She saw his eyes again as he came over her and thrust into her. She met his gaze squarely with her own, reaching for him, pulling him ever closer to her.

The bed cradled them as they began to rock and twist and writhe together.

She remembered the way they had been...

And it was nothing compared to now. Memory hadn't served so well. He could tease so sensually with the lightest brush and then move hard, and the sensation would be almost unbearable. She was achingly and acutely aware of his body...muscle, bone, every movement. He was leaner and harder than ever; his shoulders had grown broader, his abdomen tighter...he moved with a fluid fury and grace that swept her into moments of sweet oblivion, lifted her, eased her down, lifted her again...and then to a climax that seemed to shatter everything, straight down to her soul.

They lay in silence, just breathing. For a few moments, the sound was loud. It began to ease. She felt the slowing of her heartbeat; she thought that she heard his, too.

She tried to think of something to say. Something... that explained her current emotion. Something deep or profound.

She didn't speak first.

He did.

"Hmm," he said lightly. "I guess I have missed you!"

"Well," she murmured, "I'm ever so glad."

He rolled up then, looking down into her eyes. "You really are beautiful, Sarah. Inside and out, you know."

She shook her head, confused. "Just decent, I hope, like I want to believe most people in the world are."

He rolled over again, plumping up a pillow. "Oh, Sarah. So far above decent! I'd definitely rate you an eleven this evening!"

"On a scale of one to ten?"

"One to twenty."

She hit him with a pillow.

And he laughed and moved over her again, smiling. "On a scale of one to five…an eleven. Maybe a twenty or a hundred…"

He kissed her.

It had been a very, very long time.

They made love again. She thought it was dawn when they finally slept. And it was too bad. They really had so very much to do…

A killer to catch.

More murders to stop…

Including their own.

Chapter Five

Tyler was amazed that he hadn't had to drag himself out, almost crying from exhaustion. But he wasn't tired; he felt that he was wide-awake and sharp—as if some kind of new adrenaline was running through his system, something that changed the world.

Sex.

With Sarah. Different as could be…and sweet and explosive as any memory that he could begin to recall.

Biology, like breathing. Should have been. It just wasn't. Something made people come to other people and, whatever it was, it was strong. Sometimes, it became more. Sometimes it lasted forever. Sometimes it didn't.

He stood in the situation room at the precinct while the facts of the murders were laid out for the dozens of officers, agents and marshals crammed into it. All they really had were the facts that had to do with the murders—they had nothing on suspects, clues or anything at all. Dr. Layton was there, and he explained the cutting off of the heads; even some men Tyler knew to be long-timers looked a little pasty and green as they listened. Lance would be starting the second autopsy today and would soon know more. Bob Green asked Tyler to talk about their theory that Perry Knowlton might still be alive, as they knew for a fact that Archibald Lemming was dead.

Someone asked how the man could have been hiding for years and suddenly come out to commit such heinous acts. At this point, Craig asked Kieran to come forward and offer what insight she could. Tyler saw that Kieran must speak to various groups of law enforcement often; she was prepared and calm.

"As you all know, serial killers only stop when they're forced to stop. A trigger of some kind—death of a loved one, work failure, financial loss, or other traumatic losses usually start a killer off. Sometimes it's just an escalation, and it's sad but true, children who torture animals often grow up to be the next generation's serial killers. Perry Knowlton had been incarcerated for the murders of eight women in upstate New York. He and Archibald Lemming met in prison. For all intents and purposes, it appeared that Archibald killed Perry—it wouldn't have been against his nature, and he killed men and women alike. But the two might have had some kind of honor among killers—Perry Knowlton started the fight that got both men into the medical complex from which they managed to escape."

"But that doesn't answer where he's been all these years," an officer said.

"Possibly locked up."

"Fingerprints!" another agent reminded her.

"He might have been in a hospital or mental facility, or had a physical issue causing him to lie low. Or he might have been killing other places."

"Did you forget the killings at that haunted house years ago?" another officer asked, his tone derisive.

Tyler started to move forward again. He was surprised to see that Sarah had moved up to the front of the crowd, and she looked to Kieran and said, "May I?"

On Kieran's nod, Sarah took a deep breath and spoke. "I'll never forget that. I was there. With my friends. And we survived because my cousin had been taught to watch people—because people, in general, can be cruel. My uncle taught my cousin to carefully observe his surroundings and the individuals nearby. That night, he saw Archibald Lemming at the theme park before he went into the Cemetery Mansion. Lemming was alone when Davey saw him then—of course, that scenario fits if Knowlton is alive or dead.

"After Hannah Levine was murdered, I started researching everything that happened surrounding the escape. Nothing proves beyond a doubt that Perry Knowlton is dead. Also...there are over two hundred thousand unsolved homicides on the books right now in the US alone. Hannah was found in the water, so he might have been disposing of his victims in a way in which they weren't found."

There was silence around the room. Tyler was pretty sure everyone there was thinking about the one who had gotten away—their one case they couldn't crack. And it wasn't something that made them feel good.

"Thank you!" Detective Green said, moving in. "Now, get out there, officers. This killer is not going to become an 'unknown' statistic!"

"One of the police spokesmen has been briefed on what we do and don't want out for public knowledge," Craig said quietly to Tyler. "He'll handle the press conference. We can get on to the autopsy—and then over to Suzie Cornwall's building. She wasn't working. She was a patient in a clinical trial, quite seriously ill, or so her landlord told the police. The odd thing is…"

"What?" Tyler asked.

"We have a picture of her—when she was living. She really did resemble the photos we've seen of Suzie Cornwall Avery—at first glance, they might have been the same person."

Tyler was quiet for a minute. He hadn't seen Suzie in a very long time, but human nature didn't change. Suzie had always been a good, sweet soul, with a high sense of social responsibility. It wasn't going to make her feel any better, knowing that while a woman had been killed because she happened to have been given the same name at birth, that poor woman had been ill.

The stakes were high; Sarah was right. The killer was out to find those who had been there that fateful night a decade ago at the Cemetery Mansion. The night Archibald Lemming had been killed.

Revenge?

Just a sick mind?

Whichever didn't really matter. They were in danger.

"Sarah...do we bring her?"

"No, I figured she'd be comfortable with Kieran, and I have an agent staying with them at Finnegan's. They'll be fine. Trust me—if this bastard is after Sarah, he'll know by now she's with Kieran. But in my line, if there's a threat, we shoot to kill."

"I'm getting more and more worried about the others. Especially Davey."

Craig looked at him while Sarah and Kieran walked across the room to join them.

"What about this," Craig suggested. "I can have Davey and Renee brought into the city. We have an amazing safe house—easy to guard. It also has escape routes in the event the officers on duty should be killed, automatic alarms in case of a perceived danger... And my boss, Director Egan, is huge on preventing bad things. He'll want them there."

"Really?" Sarah whispered. "That leaves only Sean and Suzie, and Suzie is so terrified by what happened that she's about ready to be institutionalized!"

"They can be brought there, too. It's big. I think there are actually three separate bedrooms."

"How long can we keep them there—or keep guards on them?" Tyler asked.

"This isn't going to take long," Sarah said softly. "You will catch him soon, or..." She paused and looked at them unhappily. "Or we'll all be dead. All of us who were in the Cemetery Mansion."

In Tyler's mind, Dr. Lance Layton looked more like a mad scientist than ever. His white hair was going everywhere, half of it standing straight up on his head. He was thoughtful and energetic. "I have all kinds of tests going on. Here's the thing—poor lady was not long for the world. Poor thing! She was undergoing a new kind of cancer treatment—meant she didn't lose her hair to chemo. She had liver cancer that had spread just about through her body. Death might have been a mercy, if it hadn't been so..."

He stopped speaking. "Well, small mercy. She wouldn't have been terrified or in pain long, but would have bled out within a matter of seconds. That's something that we can truthfully tell her loved ones."

The woman had been going to die, anyway, a slow, painful death. He hoped that would help Suzie live with herself.

The police photographer, Alex Morrison, was standing by quietly. Layton looked over at him. "You're—you're getting enough?"

"I am. But the head, yes, we need a few more angles on the head."

"Right," Layton said. "Thankfully, the powers that be are concerned enough on this case to keep everyone on it working together—it's harder when you have different techs and photographers and detectives. Well, I mean, not really for me. Other than that I have to repeat my findings, though some just prefer written reports, anyway, and a written report..."

"I'm not in your way?" Morrison asked.

"No, not at all," Craig assured him.

Morrison nodded to them both and began his work.

"Thank you, Morrison. All right, down to it."

He began to drone on. Tyler listened, mentally discarding the findings that meant nothing to their investigation.

But then Dr. Layton got to the stomach contents. "Here's what's interesting. Now our first victim, Hannah Levine, had eaten hours before her death. Miss Cornwall had eaten far more recently. Both had enjoyed some prime steaks. I don't know how much that helps you, but they may have dined at the same restaurant. I know that the city is laden with steak houses."

"Interesting—a possible lead," Tyler said. "And then again, maybe they just both enjoyed steak."

Morrison, working over by the stainless steel tray that held Suzie Cornwall's head, cleared his throat. "I think I have everything we might possibly need," he said.

He looked a little flushed. Tyler certainly understood. The head no longer really resembled anything human. It hadn't been on display long, but the sun, the elements and bugs—and the violence of being chopped off—had done their share of damage. The flesh was white, red, bruised and swollen.

"Thank you, Morrison," Layton said.

"I'm sure you've been thorough," Craig said, nodding to the photographer. "I know they want to have a decent sketch out by tomorrow. The photos we found of her on social media just aren't very good. If we use them along with the images you have, an artist can come up with something that will work well in the newspapers."

"Right," Morrison said grimly. "They're going to put an image out, correct? Ask for help?"

"That's been the decision, yes," Craig told him.

The photographer nodded at them all and left quickly.

Layton continued his analysis.

They listened awhile longer, looking at the body the whole time. To his credit, even Layton, long accustomed to being the voice of the dead, seemed deeply disturbed by the remains of the murdered woman.

Then it was time to try to find out how, when and where this Suzie had met her killer.

"Oh, lord!" Sarah said.

Kieran, who had been busy with her computer, looked up.

Sarah was at her own laptop, working in Kieran's office at the psychiatric offices of Fuller and Miro. She'd intended to be busy with her current novel, *Revenge of the Martian Waspmen*, but just hadn't been able to concentrate on her distant world.

"What is it?" Kieran asked.

"I finally keyed in the right words that led me to the right sites that led me to more sites. I've found so many unsolved and bizarre murders..."

"Show me!"

Kieran walked around her desk to stand behind Sarah.

Sarah pointed and spoke softly. "This one—up in Sleepy Hollow, and chalked up to it being Sleepy Hollow. 'Headless corpse found in ravine.' Then, here. 'Hudson Valley— help needed in the murder of local bank teller,' and, when you read further, you discover that she was found in two pieces—head on a tree branch, torso in the river. Then here's another in southern Connecticut—'Skull discovered off I-95, no sign of the body.'"

"There are probably more. I'm sure Craig has his tech guy working on it," Kieran mused. She sat again. "The guy's got to be living here somewhere. Somehow. But how? He'd need a credit check to rent an apartment. He'd need to make money somehow. And he'd have to pull all this off—and manage to look like one of the crowd."

"Is that so hard in New York City?" Sarah asked. "I mean, think about it. In New York, whatever you do, don't make eye contact. We walk by dozens of down-and-outers on the streets and in the subway. A few years back, a newspaper writer did an experiment and gave one dollar to each person with a cup or a hat just on the streets. Within a mile radius, she'd given away two hundred dollars. He could have begged on the street. He could have done a dozen things. He could have robbed people—without actually killing them. No lost wallets are ever found. We're a city of tremendous wealth and the American dream, but when that fails…"

"It's a good theory," Kieran said. "We'll talk to Craig. Give me a minute!"

She disappeared and then returned to her office with Drs. Fuller and Miro in tow.

Fuller was maybe fifty, tall and extremely good-looking.

Miro was tiny, older and still attractive, with dark curly hair, a pert little gamine's face and an incredible energy that seemed to emit from her.

"Show them what you just showed me," Kieran said.

And so Sarah did. And when she was done, Fuller said, "I think you've found something. Sad to say, but in history, many people have gotten away with crimes for years. And if these killings are associated, he was careful to commit his murders in different places."

"But all close to the central point—New York City," Miro put in.

"I believe my esteemed partner and I are in agreement on this," Fuller said. "This could all be the work of one man. And," he said, pointing at Sarah's computer screen, "this is old. Dates back almost ten years. This could have been Perry Knowlton's first kill after the massacre in Cemetery Mansion."

Sarah felt a sense of panic welling in her; she wasn't afraid for herself—well, she was, of course—but she was terrified for Davey.

She looked at Kieran. "Can you make sure that my aunt and Davey are safe?"

"Absolutely," Kieran promised. "And I'll tell Craig that my good doctors have weighed in. We need to follow up on your theory. I'm not sure how, but we need to move in that direction."

EVERYONE WAS SAFE, and Sarah was extremely grateful.

"We had a cop at the house, or just outside the house, and of course I brought out coffee," Aunt Renee told Sarah. "I have to admit, I've been trying not to panic. This is…this isn't coincidence. This is terrible. If Hannah was a target, and then…seems they killed the wrong Suzie, but she was a target, and if I was to lose you and Davey, oh, my God, I'd just want to be dead myself. I can't believe this. It isn't fair. Of course, I do know," she added drily, "that life isn't fair, but still, you all survived such terror…"

Sarah gave her a big hug. Then Suzie and Sean hugged Renee, and then Davey, as their FBI guards stood back silently, letting the reunion go on.

A young woman with the leanest body Sarah had ever seen—she wondered if she even had 1 percent body fat!—came forward then. "Pizza is on its way," she said cheerfully. "We don't have any delivery here. An agent always acquires food. The Bureau has control of the entire building, with sham businesses and residences—used as office space, we're careful with taxpayer dollars!—but we want you to be relaxed enough to…well, to exist as normally as possible under the circumstances. I'm Special Agent Lawrence."

She indicated a tall man nearer the door. "That's Special Agent Parton. We're your inside crew for the moment and we work twelve-hour shifts. Our apartments are in this building—we're always on call. Tonight, however, you'll have fresh agents—nice and wide-awake, that is. The doorman and the registrar downstairs are agents, and there are two agents in the hall at all times. If you will all get together and draw up a grocery list, we'll see to getting what you need. The kitchen is there—" she pointed to the left of the front door "—and the central bath is there." She pointed to the right. "One of us will always be at that table by the door, while the other might be with you. In the very unlikely event that every agent between the entry and you is brought down, there is a dumbwaiter in the back that is really an elevator. Naturally, our engineers have worked with it—nothing manual, no pulleys or cranks. You hit a button, the door closes and it takes you down. It can't be opened on the ground level from the outside—it can only be opened from the inside once you're down there. Same button, huge and red. You can't miss it."

"This is wonderful. Thank you!" Sarah said softly.

"Catching the bad guys is our job—along with keeping the good guys alive!" Special Agent Lawrence said. "Let me show you to your rooms," she added.

The living room or parlor boasted a dual area—a TV and chair grouping to the right and a little conclave of chairs to the left. They were led down a hallway.

The bedrooms were sparse, offering just beds and dressers and small closets.

"The best place I've ever seen!" Aunt Renee said.

"This one? Can I have this one?" Davey asked, looking into one of the rooms.

They were really all the same. There had to be something slightly different for Davey to want it.

There were no windows. No way for a sniper to have a chance; no way for an outsider to see who was inside.

"Davey, whatever room you want!" Suzie said.

Davey grinned.

"What's special about it?" Sarah asked him.

"The closet is painted blue. 'Haint' blue, like they told us when my dad took me on a ghost tour in Key West. Haint blue keeps bad things away."

"Excellent," Sarah told him.

"I'll go next to Davey," Aunt Renee said.

"And we'll be across the hall," Sean agreed. "And Sarah—"

"I won't be staying. I'm going with Tyler."

Renee protested, "Oh, Sarah! The two of you should both be here—"

"Try telling a military man he needs extra protection!" Sarah said lightly. "I swear, we'll be fine."

"You're staying with Tyler?" Sean asked her. "Have you been seeing each other again? Last I heard, he was out of the military and living in Boston."

"He came because of Hannah. We'll see this through," she said.

She heard Tyler's voice; he had arrived at the safe house. It had, she realized, gotten late. She knew he and Craig had been going to the autopsy and then to interview the building owner and whatever friends— or even acquaintances—they could find of Suzie

Cornwall's, to try to trace her steps before she was taken by her killer.

"Excuse me," Sarah murmured and hurried out. He and Craig had arrived together.

She gazed at him anxiously. She didn't ask any questions; they were all in her eyes.

Tyler nodded, looking over her head, and she realized that Special Agent Lawrence, Renee, Davey, Suzie and Sean had all followed her out.

"Suzie," he said softly, "this can't make it better, I know, but the Suzie who was killed was already dying a horrible death."

"What?" she asked.

"Cancer—it had riddled her body."

"Anything else?" Sarah asked.

"We went to her building and to the hospital. No one could tell us anything. She was likable, she kept to herself. She was polite and courteous, and I'm sure we would have all liked her very much. But even her doctor said that the experimental drugs weren't having the desired effect. She was going to die a slow and horrible death."

"Poor woman, to suffer all that, and then…"

"Dr. Layton, the medical examiner, said she died quickly," Tyler said.

They were all silent. It was impossible not to wonder which would be worse—a slow and horrible death as her body decayed around her, or the horror of having her throat slit, her head sawed from her body.

"It's my fault," Suzie whispered.

"No. It's the fault of a sick and wretched killer, and

don't think anything else," Tyler said firmly. Again there was silence. Not even the agents in the room seemed to breathe.

"So," Tyler said. "We think that Perry Knowlton might still be alive. We're going to try to relive that night—together, all of us except for Hannah, of course. Try to remember what we saw in that haunted house—and if any of us might have seen Perry Knowlton."

"Might have seen him?" Sean said, confusion in his voice. "We didn't know what he looked like. Not then. I mean, later, there were pictures of him in the papers and on TV and all, but...I sure as hell didn't see him in Cemetery Mansion."

"Let's go through it. We came through at different times. Let's see what we all remember."

"It will actually be good for you all—from everything I understand from my police shrink friends, including the shrinks Kieran works with," Craig said. "And where is she, by the way?"

"She's with your partner, Mike, at Finnegan's," Special Agent Lawrence said.

"She's not a target, and Mike would die before anyone touched a hair on her head," Craig said. "Shall we?" He indicated the sitting area.

Sean and Suzie, holding hands, chose the little settee. Renee sat on one of the wingback chairs, and Tyler and Craig sat across from them. One chair was left, though there was room on the settee. "Sarah, sit," Davey said. "Sit, please."

She smiled and sat. Davey settled by her side on the floor, curling his legs beneath him.

"Davey," Tyler said, "let's start with you. You knew there was something bad going on. And I'm sorry. I know you've been through this before."

"I saw him. The bad man. Archibald Lemming," Davey said. "But I didn't know his name. My dad warned me about men like him."

"But your dad wasn't with you, whispering in your ear or anything?" Craig asked.

Davey gave him a weary look. "My dad is dead."

"Of course," Craig said, "and I'm so sorry."

"He said he would always be with me in all the good things he taught me," Davey said. "So I watch for bad people. He was bad. I saw him go in Cemetery Mansion."

"And that's why you didn't want to go in," Tyler said. He smiled at Davey. "And you warned us, but we were foolish, and we didn't listen."

"I was okay once I had my Martian Gamma Sword!" Davey said, perking up. He leaned back and looked up at Sarah. "And it was good, right?"

"It was excellent. You were a hero."

"Which is why the bad guy wants to kill me now," Davey said pragmatically.

Sarah set her hand on his shoulder.

Tyler told him, "Don't worry. We will never let that happen. So, Davey and Sarah stayed out, while Suzie, Sean, Hannah and I went in. There were people ahead of us, but the theme park was letting only a few go in at a time, so while there were people ahead and people behind, we were still more or less on our own."

"There were motion-activated animatronic characters everywhere," Suzie said. "I remember that."

"I remember when we were going in, the 'hostess' character stationed there—a French maid, I think—was acting strangely." Tyler went on. "I don't think she knew anything then, but I'm sure she felt as if something was odd. Maybe she was bright enough to have a premonition of some kind—maybe someone was late or early or had gone in or hadn't gone in. She seemed strange. Which, of course, would have been normal, since it was a haunted house."

"I remember that, too," Sean said. "As a high school senior I couldn't admit it, but…yeah, I was scared. But you know, we were part of the football team back then. We couldn't be cowards."

Suzie was nodding. "Honestly? I think—even though we were assholes about Davey not wanting to go in—I think we were a little unnerved from the get-go. Then there was the massive character in the music room. Very tall, and blond. That automaton, or whatever. Scared the hell out of me."

"What?" Sarah asked. "An automaton?"

"You couldn't have missed it," Suzie said. "Seriously, it was tall. Over six feet. It was creepy. Really freaked me out."

Sarah frowned. "You know, we talked to the cops, we talked to each other…and still, sometimes, it's like I remember new things. Maybe even my nightmares, I'm not sure. Honestly, I know we were almost running from the start, but when Davey and I came through, there was no character. There were no figures in the music room. Who could have moved an automaton in that kind of time? Especially a big one?"

Tyler leaned forward. "I remember it clearly—I remember how it scared Suzie horribly. It was definitely there."

"And when Davey and I came through, there was definitely not a character there," Sarah said.

"He was sitting at the piano," Suzie insisted.

"Not when we came through," Sarah said.

"Maybe it…"

"What? Just disappeared?" Sean asked her.

"But—I was so sure it was an automaton! It—it talked to me!" Suzie said. "Oh, my God! He saw me that night. He saw my face clearly. And yet… he killed another woman." Suzie stared at Tyler and Craig hopefully. "Was it possibly accidental? Was she old, was she…different…was she…not like me?"

"I'm sorry, Suzie. She wasn't your twin, but…"

"But he saw me over a decade ago. People change," Suzie said harshly. She sighed. "Okay, fine, so much for that theory. He meant to kill me. To behead me. To saw my head off!"

She started to sob. Sean pulled her close.

"Don't cry, Suzie," Davey said. "He wants to kill all of us. And he's a terrible person. None of it is your fault."

"Poor Hannah…but could it be? Could it really be?" Suzie whispered.

"Him," Davey said somberly.

They all looked at him. He had propped his elbows on his knees, folded his hands and rested his chin upon his knuckles. He looked like an all-seeing wise man.

"Him, the other killer, the bad guy," Davey said. He shook his head. "Yes, I think he was the other bad guy. If you saw him. He was gone when Sarah and I came through. He was gone, because he knew. The one guy—Archibald Lemming. He was meant to die. But his friend, the one everyone thought was dead—he meant to live. He was there that night, but he got away. It would have been easy. Everyone was screaming and running. Yes. It is him, right? He killed Hannah. And he's still out there, right? He's the one who is trying to kill all of us."

There was silence.

Then Tyler told Davey, "But you knew, Davey. You saved us then. And you know now, and so you're going to help us all save ourselves now." He smiled. "Because your dad taught you to be smart. He taught you to know people, which is something we who don't have Down syndrome don't always do."

Davey smiled back at him.

"Mom is good, too. Dad taught her to be a little bit Down syndrome."

Renee smiled and nodded. "Yep. I'm a little bit Down syndrome, thanks to your dad. He was a very good man."

Davey straightened proudly.

Tyler turned and looked at Craig. "I think that must be it—the character who was there, and then wasn't. Archibald Lemming didn't kill Perry Knowlton. I think maybe Lemming had a death wish—but he wanted to go out with a bang. Lemming had some kind of insider info about escaping through the infirmary. They killed personnel to escape, but even then they had to have timing information and all. So, say that Knowlton was the brains behind the escape. And then they found Haunted Hysteria. What a heaven on earth for someone who wanted blood and terror!"

"And all these years," Suzie said, "he's been just watching? Waiting? Is that possible?"

Sarah said softly, "We think he has been busy. Yes, he's been in New York City. This is theory, of course. But we've done some research. We think he's still been murdering people. He just takes little jaunts out of the city to kill."

"Oh, my God!" Suzie said.

"But now," Tyler said, "he's killing here. Right in the city."

"Revenge," Sarah said.

"But…he lived!" Suzie protested.

"Yes, but he might have idolized Lemming. And while he's a killer, and he's been killing, this is different. He's been imitating Lemming, but not making a huge display out of his crimes. But now…who knows? Maybe he was careful, but then saw Hannah on the street or something. Maybe he was just biding his time. But the thing is, now…"

"Now?" Suzie breathed.

Sarah looked at Tyler. "And now we have to have our justice—before he gets his revenge!"

Chapter Six

The safe house wasn't far from Finnegan's, making it simple to leave and head to Broadway and the pub. Kieran had gone there to help out, which she often did when she was anxious and waiting for Craig.

But by the time Sarah and Tyler reached Finnegan's, it had grown quiet and Kieran was back in the office. Declan, Kevin and Danny, Sarah had learned, had become accustomed to having their office turned into a conference room for Craig and Kieran when something other than inventory and payroll needed to be attended to.

An undercover agent, someone who worked with Craig, was sitting at the bar, watching the crowd while sipping a Kaliber, Guinness's entry on the nonalcoholic side of beer.

He greeted them with a friendly nod when they arrived. Declan, behind the bar, cheerfully sent them to the office. Kieran was at the desk.

"Everyone is good—safe?" Kieran asked as they entered and took up chairs in front of the desk.

"Safe and sound," Sarah said. "I'm just so glad

Davey is there now. I have a feeling that Perry Knowlton must know Davey was the key to ending everything that night."

"Maybe not," Tyler said. "He didn't try for Davey first."

"No, he went for Hannah, who, sad to say, was an easy target. She wouldn't have recognized him, but maybe he recognized her. And she would have been an easy first mark because…because she would see men. She was working as a hooker," Sarah said sadly.

"And that makes sense—go for the easiest victim first," Kieran said, nodding.

"And we think we have a lead, though where it can take us, I don't know," Tyler said.

Craig went on to explain what they'd discussed.

"And no one really saw him, right? What he really looked like?" asked Kieran.

"I never saw him at all, and neither did Davey. We think he was pretending to be an automaton in the music room. From what they said, he scared Suzie half to death when they went through. But there was no such person—or automaton—by the time Davey and I arrived. He could have run out already—or he could have gone through any one of half a dozen emergency exits."

"But his picture was in the papers, on the web and TV screens, right?" Kieran asked.

"Yes, of course," Tyler said. "I did see him. He was very distinctive. Tall, at least my height. And lean. With a long face with sharp cheekbones and jaw."

"Well, at least not a medium height—someone

who blends in with the crowd. But there are a lot of men over six feet in New York City," Craig said.

"Maybe you should be staying at the safe house," Kieran said thoughtfully.

"No," Sarah said.

"Well, Tyler, too—he's one of you," Kieran pointed out.

Tyler shook his head. "I think Sarah and I will be all right. If he comes for one of us, it's going to be when we're alone. He isn't going to come to a hotel room. He doesn't kill with a gun, but with a knife. I have a gun. And it's always best to bring a gun to a knife fight. As long as you're steady, the gun is going to win every time."

"And we should have something to work with soon enough," said Craig. He looked at Sarah and nodded an acknowledgment. "Sarah had it right, we think, from the beginning. We found no less than ten unsolved murders that had to do with total or near decapitation, ranging from Westchester County— Hudson Valley and the Sleepy Hollow area, as Sarah found—to Connecticut and New Jersey. Regional police are sending us everything they have on those killings. We'll be able to go over them tomorrow. But most importantly, our tech department has entered the last known picture of Perry Knowlton into the computer. Tomorrow, we'll be starting off the day with images of what Perry Knowlton might look like now, and we're putting out pictures of Hannah and Suzie. Hopefully, someone might come forward, having seen them somewhere. Our appeal to the public will contain a subtle warning, of course. No one is safe while this man is at work."

"We should call it a night," Kieran said. "And get started again in the morning. I have a court appearance at nine, so I'll be out part of the day. Sarah, you should hang at the safe house during that time."

Sarah knew she probably should. That fear did live within her somewhere.

But she was going to be with Tyler.

She smiled. "I'll be safe," she promised.

Everyone stood. Out in the bar and dining area, they said good-night to Declan, the only one of Kieran's siblings still working.

Tyler and Sarah were silent as they drove to the hotel. The valet took the car; the hotel lobby was quiet. There was no one in the elevator with them.

"You think we're really safe here?"

"I think I'll shoot first and ask questions later," Tyler said.

She smiled.

"You should think about going to the safe house," he told her quietly. "It's one thing for me to take chances with my life, but...I'm not so sure you should have that kind of faith in me."

"I have ultimate faith in you."

That night, she didn't have to join him in the shower. The door was barely closed, his gun and holster were barely laid by the bed before he had her in his arms, before they were both busy grasping at one another's clothing and dropping it to a pile on the floor. His kisses had become pure fire, heated, demanding, like a liquid blaze that seemed to engulf her limbs and everything in between. She returned his hunger ravenously, anxious to be flush with him, to feel his flesh with every inch of her own, feel the vital life beneath that skin, muscle, bone, heartbeat, breath…

He pressed her down to the bed and made love to her with those hot liquid kisses…all down the length of her body. The world faded away in a sea of pure sensation. She crawled atop him, kissing, touching, loving, as if she would never have enough.

And then they were together, he was in her, and the sensation was so keen she could barely keep from crying out, alerting the world to their whereabouts and exactly what they were doing.

She bit her lip, soaring on a wave of sheer ecstasy. All that lay between them seemed to burst with a show of light before her eyes, a field of stars and color. Then she drifted into the incredibly sweet sensation of climax as it swept over her and shook her with a flow of little shudders and spasms. And then they were still, with the incredible sense of warmth and comfort and ease, her just lying beside him.

She felt she should speak; she didn't want to. They'd been this close once before, when life had been all but Utopia.

But everything had changed. He'd said that she'd left him—but he had been the one to walk away. Move away. Start a completely new life.

He pulled her close to him.

She thought he might speak.

He did not. He just held her, his lips brushing her forehead as they lay there.

She stared into the darkness for a long time, not sleeping.

There was sound. The slightest sound in the hallway.

Tyler was out of bed, his Smith and Wesson in his hands, before she could really register the noise. He went to the door. And then he came back, returning the gun to the side of the bed. Sliding in beside her, he told her, "Two girls in 708 returning from a night at the bar. They're trying to be quiet—kind of surprising one of them hasn't knocked the other over yet!"

She smiled. This time, when he pulled her close, they made love again.

And then she did drift to sleep.

She thought she would dream of sandy beaches, a warm sun and a balmy breeze—and Tyler at her side.

Instead, she dreamed of a tall dark man lurking in the shadows, watching her. She was back in Cemetery Mansion, racing after Davey, trying to stop him. And she was in the music room, with no one else there, and it seemed no matter how fast she ran, she couldn't reach the dining room, couldn't find Davey, couldn't get out. And though she couldn't really see him, she knew that he was there. The tall dark man.

Watching her.

Calculating when it would be her turn.

TYLER HAD NEVER needed much sleep, and he was glad of it. At just about six in the morning, he woke; at his side, Sarah was twisting and turning.

He whispered to her, pulling her closer to him, not wanting to wake her, but not wanting her to suffer through whatever was going on in her dreams—or nightmares. He wanted to ease whatever plagued her, even while he marveled at being with her once again. Her body was so smooth and sleek, curved upon the snow-white sheets. Her hair had always been a sunny shade of gold, and it fell around her like a mantle.

"Sarah," he said gently.

Her eyes opened. For a moment, they were wide and frightened—just for a moment. And then she saw his face, and she smiled and flushed.

"Nightmare," she murmured.

"So I gathered. About?"

"Cemetery Mansion," she said softly. "You know, sometimes it takes me a few minutes to remember what I had for lunch the day before—but I remember everything about that awful night."

"So do I."

"Do you ever...dream?"

"I've had some dreadful nightmares, yeah, for sure."

She sighed. "I'm glad to hear it. I mean—I'm not glad you have nightmares. I'm glad I'm not the only one. I guess that's not really very nice, either!"

"You're human."

She stared at him for a moment, blue eyes still very wide, but her expression grim. "Human. So is this killer. He's human—and he's done these things!"

Tyler was silent a minute. Then he told her, "There's something wrong with people like Archibald Lemming and Perry Knowlton. You know that—you've been around Kieran enough. When they get to such a point, it's a fine distinction between psychopaths or sociopaths—whatever wiring they have in their heads, it's not normal. In a sense, they've lost all their sense of humanity. The normal person is heartsick to hear about an earthquake that killed hundreds, but this killer would want the pictures. He would relish the death and destruction. He would wish that it had been his handiwork."

She shook her head. "I can't feel sorry for him. He's sick, but after what he's done to people…that kind of sickness doesn't draw any sympathy from me. I guess it should, but it doesn't."

"The thing is…even if he were to finish this bit of revenge—"

"You mean, kill all of us."

"Even if he were to finish, he wouldn't stop. It's impossible to know now if he did commit any or all of the unsolved crimes you and the FBI found. It's impossible to know if he was gearing up, practicing for this—or if, in his warped mind, he realized that he should take his desire to kill and turn it into revenge."

"He's got to be stopped!" she whispered.

"He's careful. Hannah was an easy target. He found Suzie Cornwall—the wrong Suzie Cornwall—and lured her off alone easily enough. But now we're onto him. And he'll figure that out. I don't think he intends to take any chances, so we have to keep the others at the safe house and be incredibly alert and aware ourselves."

He heard his phone buzzing—it was time to be up and moving.

He reached for his cell. He wasn't surprised the caller was Craig.

"The pictures are about to go out."

"That's good."

"Yes, but you have to know something."

"What is that?"

He heard a bit of commotion. The next thing he knew, Craig was gone and Kieran was on the phone.

"Tyler! He's been at Finnegan's. This man…this man who appears to be Perry Knowlton…he's been at Finnegan's several times. I'm not there all the time so I don't really know, but…I've seen him! I've seen him at least three times!"

IT WAS EARLY and that meant there was no problem for Declan to open the pub just for friends and family. His siblings along with his fiancée, Mary Kathleen, and Craig, Tyler and Sarah sat around two tables that they'd pushed together, drinking coffee.

Sarah made sure Tyler was introduced to Kevin, Kieran's twin—the one brother he'd not met yet. Kevin couldn't stay long; he was shooting a "Why I Love New York" commercial for the tourist board at ten.

"We shouldn't have asked you to come in," Tyler said. "Nice to meet you—and I'm sorry."

"It's all right. Declan called me as soon as he received the message from Craig with the police computer rendering of Perry Knowlton. I never waited on him, but I know I've seen the bastard in here."

"It's frightening—and interesting. Because if you recognize him, hopefully others will, too," Tyler said.

Craig had printouts of the composite lying on the table. He told them, "Perry Knowlton is forty-three years old now. He started his killing binge at the age of twenty-nine, and was convicted of five murders and incarcerated by the time he was thirty-one."

Tyler picked up the account. "In prison, he met Archibald Lemming, and they probably compared their methods for finding their victims—and for killing them."

"And," Kieran continued, "they would remember their crimes. They were probably thrilled to have someone to tell, trying to one-up each other all the time. They liked to enjoy their memories over and over again—just as others would enjoy talking about their vacation to Italy, or a day at a beautiful beach."

Declan tapped the image of Perry Knowlton that lay on the table. "A few times before—and then less than two weeks ago—he was at the end of the bar. He ordered whiskey, neat. He was polite and even seemed to be charming those around him. Easy, level voice."

"You're sure it was him?" Tyler asked.

"I'd bet a hell of a lot on it," Declan said.

"And I'm damned sure, too," Kevin said.

"He was at a table, maybe a month ago," Mary Kathleen told them all. "And he was quite amicable, very nice, complimented the potato soup and the shepherd's pie."

"I served him when he was hanging around with a number of the regulars," Danny said. "He had them all laughing."

"The all-around guy-next-door," Kieran murmured. "Historically, there have been several truly charismatic serial killers, the poster boy being Ted Bundy. He worked for a suicide crisis center, for God's sake, with Anne Rule—long before he was infamous for his crimes and she was famous for her books. But he wasn't the only one. I don't know that everyone would have fallen for Charles Manson, but he knew how to collect the young and disenfranchised. Andrew Cunanan—Versace's killer—was supposedly intelligent and affable. Paul John Knowles was known as the 'Casanova Killer.' The list can go on, but…"

"A charming, bright, handsome psychopath," Sarah murmured. "Great."

"But he's been exposed now," Tyler reminded her. "Someone knows him. Someone has seen him and knows his habits."

"Oh, aye, and sure!" Mary Kathleen said. "He likes good shepherd's pie, tips well enough and has lovely laughing green eyes. Ah, but how they must look when—" She broke off, shivering. "Horrible. Don't just shoot him. Skin him alive, saw him to pieces!" she said passionately.

Sarah set her hand on Mary Kathleen's. "But that's what makes the difference between us…" she said. "We wouldn't do those things to another human being. Although I understand completely what you're saying. I was there. The idea that killers find a little torture themselves does have its appeal."

"Do any of you remember the first time you saw him—and the last time?" Tyler asked.

"The first time..." Declan mused.

"Last October!" Mary Kathleen said. "Oh, I do remember—because I had to leave early that day. Me niece was coming over from Dublin. He offered to pay his check quickly."

"That was nearly five months ago," Kieran murmured.

"Do you think he's been looking for Sarah all that time?" Kevin asked.

"How would he have known that she worked here at all?" Declan murmured.

"He might have found her by accident. He might have seen her one day and followed her... It's a huge city, but we all know that sometimes it can be a very small world. And it's easy to discover personal details on social media," Tyler said.

"My address was never out anywhere!" Sarah said firmly.

"Of course not," Declan said. "But you might have written something about the pub. And that brought him here."

"Maybe," she murmured.

"He must have figured out after the first month or so that she wasn't working here anymore," Declan commented flatly. "But..."

Craig's phone rang and he excused himself.

"He thought that she'd come back," Tyler said. "He

knew you worked here at some time or another, Sarah. And when was the last time anyone saw him?"

"Like I said," Declan told him. "Ten days to two weeks ago. Sorry I can't be more definite."

"He knows some things, but obviously not enough," Kieran said, looking at Sarah. "He didn't know Suzie wasn't using Cornwall anymore—he didn't know she and Sean Avery were married. He tries to find what he's looking for, but he hasn't the resources he'd surely love to have. That means we've got an edge on him," she added softly.

"Director Egan called," Declan told them. He was, Sarah knew, Craig's direct boss. "He says he'll keep Josh McCormack in here, watching over us and the pub, during opening hours. We are licensed to have a gun, which is behind the bar. But only the family has access."

"Oh! If something were to happen to someone in the pub, or to Finnegan's... I'm so sorry I seem to have brought this on you!" Sarah said.

"You didn't," Declan said. "We're tough. We'll manage, as we always have."

"Sláinte!" Mary Kathleen said, raising her coffee cup.

Smiles went around; coffee mugs were lifted in cheers.

Craig returned to the table. "Tyler, there's been a break in the case. The bartender at Time and Time Again also recognized Perry Knowlton from the composite. I think we should talk to him again."

"Ready when you are," Tyler said, standing. He looked down at Sarah.

"Hell, no," she said. "I'm not staying anywhere. I'm coming with you."

WHEN THEY REACHED the bar in the theater district, Detective Bob Green and his photographer, Alex Morrison, were already there.

Tyler almost ran into Morrison. "Hey, you all made it," the man said, watching him curiously. "There are no security cameras here, so they want pictures of the bar and the entry. Seems our fellow Knowlton liked to hang around here a lot. He flirted with Hannah— sorry, you can talk to the bartender yourselves. I'll get on with it."

He seemed to be taking pictures of all aspects of the bar.

The place was still closed; it was ten thirty and Tyler imagined it opened by eleven or eleven thirty. They needed the time alone with Luke, the bartender.

Luke was already talking to Detective Green, who was seated on one of the bar stools. He saw Sarah coming and smiled and waved—obviously a bit taken with her. That was good; she had said she could be helpful, and though Tyler really wanted her safely far away from the action, she was useful. So far, she'd actually garnered far more info than he had, just by being friendly and curious, and he was supposedly the investigator.

Luke greeted them all and offered them coffee.

For once, Tyler thought he'd been coffee'd out.

"I should have been able to meet you wherever," Luke said. "I don't usually work days, but…the other bartender quit. She saw the picture and she just quit. That guy's been in here lots. He was teasing and flirting with Hannah the night…the night she…the night she was murdered. But can it really be him? He seems really decent. Nice—he tips big, unlike a hell of a lot of people around here. Are you sure that it's him?"

"We're sure we need to find him," Tyler said.

"Have you seen him since Hannah was killed?" Sarah asked.

"Oh, yes."

"Yes?" Tyler asked.

"Hell, he was in here last night! And, I mean, until the news this morning, I had no clue. No clue at all. I was nice, he was nice. Oh, God, he's good-looking, you know. Flirtatious. He talked to so many girls. I just hope…oh, God! I hope none of them turn up dead!"

"We're hoping that, too," Craig said.

Detective Bob Green looked at Craig. "You guys are handling the safe house. We'll see to a watch on this place."

"He won't come back here now," Sarah said.

"Well, he's pretty cocky," Luke said.

Sarah shook his head. "He didn't think that we'd know it was him—but now he knows we're looking for him, thanks to the picture we released to the press. I think he'll lie low for a while. But hey, sure—keep an eye on the bar."

"We don't have a hell of a lot else," Green said.

"She's right, though."

Tyler swung around. It was the photographer, Alex, who had spoken, and he was now coming up to join them. He flushed and said, "Hey, I'm with the forensic unit—civilian. Not a cop. But I've taken a hell of a lot of photos, and…well, here. Here's some of what I got at the park the other day. The park where Suzie Cornwall was found. If you look…"

He held his camera forward, twisting it around so that they could gather close and see the images right-side up.

"We're looking at the body of Suzie Cornwall in situ," Green said.

"Yes, yes, but I just realized what else I have here—studying it all. Let me enlarge it for you… Look at the people," Alex said. He clicked a side button; the image honed in on the crowd, growing larger.

And there he was.

Perry Knowlton, aged just as the computer suggested he would age.

Tall, with a headful of blond hair. Lean face, rugged chin, broad, high brow. Lean, long physique. Tall, yes, standing next to a rabbi with a tall hat—and a guy who looked like a lumberjack. He almost blended in with the crowd.

"He does come back to the scene of the crime," Sarah murmured.

"He's been everywhere!" Alex murmured. "He's been here. God knows, the man might have been in the city since the Cemetery Mansion massacre."

"You remember the massacre?" Sarah asked him.

"Anyone who was in the city at the time remembers it," Detective Green said.

"Some more than others," Tyler said, studying Alex. "Were you at the theme park?"

"Yeah. Oh, yeah, I was already there—when I was called in to work for the local unit that night! I was still so raw—I'd made it into the academy, but one time when I was sitting around sketching to pass the time, a colleague told me they were short in the forensic department. My curiosity was tweaked, and I figured I could always come back and finish the academy. I never did, but…anyway. I wasn't making any kind of big bucks, if you know what I mean, so I was moonlighting, too. Working part-time for the amusement company. That night, I was working as a float—you know, I was sent wherever they were missing an employee or actor. That night I was a ticket taker, not far from where the Cemetery Mansion had been erected. I can't believe I was there—that I might have seen the creepy bastard go running by me—as he escaped. I just remember the blood and the screams and the people who were so terrified, running, running, running…" He stopped, shaking his head. "Hell, I'd give my eyeteeth to help in catching this bastard, so anything—anything at all I can do to help, I'm there. I'm going to go back over the pictures we took of the crime scene when we found Hannah Levine…you know, um, both places where they found her…head and torso."

"Interesting," Tyler said. "Maybe you can find some kind of a distinguishing something about him that will give us a clue as to where he's been living—he has to be in the city somewhere."

"He wears black in these pictures," Alex commented. "A black coat."

"He wears a black coat when he's in here, too," said Luke. He cleared his throat. "Do you think he will come back here? I mean, I should be okay, right? He's going after women."

Alex Morrison was flicking through his digital pictures. Tyler reached for the camera.

He'd just recently been taking shots of the place. The large, etched mirror behind the bar; the old wooden stools; the rather shabby booths out on the floor; and the tables there. He had taken pictures of the tables inside and of the outside of the establishment.

A large canopy awning hung down over the front of the building, though it hadn't become a warm enough spring yet for patrons to want to sit outside. Or even have a window open.

But Alex Morrison had taken pictures outside, of the streets leading east and west of the bar. He had caught other buildings in his shots.

And he'd caught a number of pedestrians.

Tyler studied the pictures. He felt Sarah's hand on his shoulder; she was looking over at them, as well.

Mostly, it appeared to be Manhattan's daily business crowd—rushing here, there, trying to get to work on time.

People were in line at the coffee shop toward the corner.

A woman had paused to adjust her shoe.

Tyler glanced up at Alex Morrison. He was probably just in his early to midthirties now.

Tyler vaguely remembered him as the photographer back then, but they hadn't had any real contact at the time. But Morrison had been decent, straightforward, yet gentle due to their ages.

However, not as brave or passionate as he seemed to be now.

His photos were good. He had an eye for focus and detail.

"Touch here, and you can enlarge wherever you want," Alex told them.

"Thanks."

"Go back a few," Sarah said. "There's a really great long shot. It brings in the street, going toward the Times Square area."

Tyler flicked back.

And at first, he saw nothing unusual.

No details at all. And then he paused.

There was a woman in the road. The street wasn't closed to traffic, but she was jaywalking and in the middle of the road as cars went by her.

All around her, neon lights blazed—even in the morning.

The pictures hadn't been taken an hour ago. Some had just been taken as Alex had entered the bar.

Tyler touched the screen as Alex had shown him. The image enlarged.

She was wearing a white dress, white coat and low

white pumps. She had a bobbed platinum haircut—
like Marilyn Monroe.

He could see that, compared to other people walking in the vicinity, she was tall. Really tall.

"She..." Green murmured.

"Oh, Lord!" Sarah said.

"What is it?" Alex Morrison asked them, frowning as he turned the viewing screen back toward himself.

"She is a he," Tyler said quietly. "She is Perry Knowlton. When did you snap that?"

"That's...that's one of the last images I took—maybe ten minutes ago."

Tyler was up and heading out before the others could blink.

No.

She was a he, and the "he" was Perry Knowlton.

And he was out there, close.

Closer than they had ever imagined.

Chapter Seven

Sarah sat tensely on her bar stool.

Tyler had raced out; Craig rose, but hesitated.

"Go on—one of us should go, too, and hell, you're younger than I am, if you're going to be running around!" Detective Green said. "I'll stick here. Alex is with me."

Then Craig was out the door.

"He won't be there anymore," Alex said dismally.

"It hasn't been much time. And he's a tall man in drag. They have a chance at finding him," Detective Green said.

Alex shrugged; it was apparent he sincerely doubted that.

"He's picked up new talents," Sarah said.

"What do you mean?" Alex asked.

"I've been reading a lot about him. Loner. Had an alcoholic, abusive father, but I really wonder what that might have meant. He was very young when he was apparently discovered cutting up little creatures in the park. And then..."

"So, what new habit?" Alex asked.

She smiled. "I guess he learned at Cemetery Mansion about costumes. There was nothing in his earlier history about him dressing up to perform any of his atrocities—or even to go and view the fruit of his labor. Nothing about wearing women's clothes."

As she spoke, her phone rang. It was Tyler. Her heart leaped with a bit of hope that he'd called to tell her they'd taken Perry Knowlton down.

Really, too much to hope.

"He's not on the street, but we're not ready to give up," he said. "I'm going to ask Detective Green to get you to the safe house. You can spend a little time with Davey and everyone."

She bit her lip. She didn't really want to go; she liked working with him and Craig—questioning people, listening.

But she couldn't keep Detective Green sitting here all day on a bar stool.

And she knew it was unsafe for her to stay alone.

"Sarah, is that all right?"

"Of course," she said. She handed the phone to Bob Green.

She heard Tyler's voice speaking, and then Green told him, "I'm going to get some men on the street, as well, but…we know now Perry Knowlton is capable of being a changeling. He could be anything and anywhere by now."

Sarah could hear Tyler's answer. "But that's just it—we are aware now. That makes a difference."

"I'll see Sarah to the safe house. More officers will

be out immediately—I'll join the manhunt when I've made sure Sarah is with the others."

He hung up and handed the phone back to her. "I'll get you there now, in my car."

"You're going to leave already?" Luke asked, looking unnerved. "Someone needs to be… Am I safe?"

"He's on the run. He won't come back here," Green replied.

Luke swallowed. He looked at Sarah and said, "Um, come visit some other time, huh? We're not usually such a bad place. I'm…"

The detective had already risen. Luke was actually looking a little ashen, and Green clamped a hand on his shoulder. "You're okay. I will have a patrolman on his way here. You're going to be okay."

PERRY KNOWLTON WAS tall and blond and had ice-cold dark green eyes.

Which really meant nothing now. Eye color could easily be changed with contacts. Hair color was as mercurial as the tide.

He couldn't change his height.

They started where Alex Morrison's digital images had last shown him.

Craig took the right side of the street.

Tyler took the left.

He entered a popular chain dress store. A number of shoppers were about, but he quickly saw the cashier's booth toward the middle front of the store.

"I'm looking for a woman, very tall, platinum hair,

in a white dress," he told the young clerk. "Have you seen her?"

"Oh, yes! Your friend came in just a few minutes ago. She's trying on maxi dresses. I helped her find a size."

Tyler smiled. "She's still here?"

"Dressing rooms are at the back."

"Thanks!"

Tyler hurried to the rear of the store. There was a row of fitting rooms, five in all. Only one was in use; he looked at the foot-long gap at the bottom of the doors.

Someone was standing in a pool of white.

The white dress?

He drew his gun and kicked open the door.

A middle-aged woman, quite tall, with a fine-featured face, stared at him in shock.

"I'm so sorry. Oh, Lord, I'm so sorry—I'm after a killer," he said. Hell. That sounded lame; he was just so damned desperate to catch Perry Knowlton.

He was so damned close.

Now he might well be close to a lawsuit.

"I'm so sorry, honestly."

She smiled at him. "Sure, honey. But hey, you're the best excitement I've had in some time. I guess that was a gun in your pocket! Hi—I'm Myrna!"

THE FBI SAFE HOUSE was really pretty incredible. Entering was like going into one of the hundreds of skyscrapers in the city. They had to check in at the door;

the girl at the desk appeared to be a clerk. She was, of course, an agent.

And Sarah was aware that the man reading the paper in the lobby was an agent, as well.

They were given permission to go up. Bob Green paused to have a conversation with the agents on duty at the door. There was complete local-federal trust on this case with those involved, but there was still a conversation.

Aunt Renee was in the kitchen; she'd invited their FBI guardians to her very special French toast brunch that morning, and she was busy cooking away when Sarah arrived. "All done soon! Suzie and Sean are going to join us." She smiled lamely. "It's not so bad here," she said softly. "I wish you were hiding out with us, but…I do understand. As long as you're careful. Davey…Davey is in his room. He's doing okay. He understands."

"Of course he understands," Sarah said. She smiled. "He usually does. He plays us when he chooses!"

"I guess so," Renee said softly. "Sometimes, I wonder if I'm overprotective. But the thing is, there are cruel people in this world. Well, as we know, there are heinous crazy killers, but…I mean in general. Grade school children can be especially unkind, making fun of anyone who is even a little bit different. And there are adults…they may not even be bad people, but… they don't know how to manage. Honestly, sometimes neighbors will walk on the other side of the street if they see me coming with Davey. I need to let some of the good in. Odd thing to realize when you're hiding from a killer, huh?"

Renee smiled ruefully at her. Sarah bit her lip lightly and nodded.

She was overprotective of Davey, too. And, yes, the world could be cruel—besides sadistic killers. But it wasn't a bad thing to protect those you loved.

Maybe it was just bad to assume others didn't love them equally.

"I'll go see how he's doing," Sarah said.

"He loves you, you know."

"And I love him."

"He loves Tyler, too."

"And I know that Tyler loves him."

Renee nodded. "Tyler does love him. He really does."

"Breakfast smells divine," she said. "Is it still breakfast?"

"Brunch!" Renee said.

"Yes, brunch sounds great. There's enough?"

"You know me. There's enough to feed a small army!"

Sarah left her aunt and headed to the room Davey had chosen. She tapped on the door and he told her to come in.

He was sitting cross-legged on the bed, with his computer.

He looked up at her. "I miss my girlfriend!"

"Of course you do. She's a sweetie. But I'll bet she understands."

He nodded. Then he said, "No, not really." He shrugged. "Her mama doesn't even want me talking to her now. Maybe…"

"It will be all right. You called Tyler in, and my friends, Kieran and her boyfriend, FBI Special Agent Frasier—they're all working on it. It's going to be okay."

"It will be okay," Davey said with certainty. He reached behind his back. "I still have my Martian Gamma Sword!"

"Of course. You made it okay once."

He nodded. "You just have to know."

"We didn't see him, Davey. The others saw him. Perry Knowlton, I mean."

"But he knows. I'm so sorry he hurt Hannah. And the other woman."

Sarah was sure no one had described the grisly murders to Davey. Of course, there were TVs just about everywhere.

And Davey loved his computer.

"No more haunted houses," Davey said.

"No. Definitely not."

"Bad people use whatever they can."

"That's true, Davey." Sarah kissed his cheek. "We can all learn from you!" she said softly. "You have that Martian Gamma Sword ready. You just never know."

"You just never know," he agreed.

"What are you doing on the computer? Have

you been able to talk to Megan through My Special Friends or any other site?"

He nodded, a silly little smile teasing his face. "Yeah, I talk to Megan. I love Megan."

"I'm very happy for you."

"It's forever kind of love," he said sagely.

"That's nice."

"Like Tyler," he said.

"Oh, Davey. I know…what you did was very manipulative, and yet…"

He grinned. "I think that's better than devious!"

"Well, anyway, it's good that Tyler is here. For now. But please don't count on forever, okay?"

But Davey shook his head. "Forever," he said.

"I think I'm going to go and see if I can help your mom. I got here in time for brunch. Cool, huh? You like being here, right?"

"I'm okay," he said.

He was looking at his screen again. She didn't know if he was trying to communicate with his girlfriend or if he was studying movies—looking up actors and directors.

At the doorway she paused, glancing back at him. "Tell Megan I said hi, okay?"

"I will. I'm not talking to Megan right now."

"What are you doing?"

He looked up at her, a strange expression on his face.

It wasn't mean. Davey didn't have a mean bone in his body, and in a thousand years he would never purposely hurt anyone.

"Davey?"

He smiled then, his charming little smile. "Research!" he told her.

"On?"

"On…whatever I find!"

"Ah. Well, breakfast—I mean brunch!—soon."

She left him and headed out to help her aunt. She wondered, even then, if she shouldn't check out just what he was researching on his computer.

IF HE'D BEEN going to burst in on someone other than the killer he was trying to catch, Tyler had at least chosen the right person.

Myrna was Myrna Simpson, and it just happened that she was the wife of retired police lieutenant August Simpson. While Tyler had awkwardly tried to explain himself, she waved a hand. "Please, don't. I'm fine. No big deal."

"Thank you!" he told her and turned to walk away.

"I believe I know who you're after!" she said. "Tall woman—actually an inch or so taller than me. Very blonde. A drag queen? Or…just someone in costume?"

"Someone in costume, we believe."

"Too bad. He'd make a great drag queen," Myrna said. "He bought some things. I saw a few of them, but the clerk can probably give you a real list."

"The clerk said he was still in the dressing room."

"Two clerks are working. Mindy and Fiona. Come on."

It turned out he'd spoken to Mindy. Fiona hadn't

been at the desk. She was then, though, a woman older than Mindy and the manager on duty.

She was suspicious at first. Tyler gave her his ID, but she remained skeptical, even with Myrna Simpson trying to help out.

Luckily, Craig Frasier walked in. His FBI identification made Fiona much more agreeable.

She gave them a list of the purchases made by Perry Knowlton.

"Is she here often?" Tyler asked.

"Often enough, I guess. Every couple of weeks," Mindy said.

When they finished, Tyler thanked Myrna again. "You really had no reason to trust me, but you did."

She laughed. "I told you. I've been married to a cop—now retired—for thirty-three years. I learned a lot about sizing up people with first impressions. Though, to be honest, I mistook your man, Perry Knowlton, for someone with a few issues—not a serial killer. If I see him anywhere, I'll be in touch."

IN THE KITCHEN of the safe house, Aunt Renee had just about finished her special French toast.

"Want to set the table?" she asked Sarah.

After she set places, Sarah headed over to Special Agents Lawrence and Parton, who were by the door, diligently on guard.

"Brunch!" she told them.

"I'll stay. You eat first," Parton told Lawrence.

"You sure?"

"Just make sure you leave me some!" He glanced

at his watch, then looked up and grinned at Sarah. "Sorry. We've been on a long shift. Reinforcements are coming in an hour or so."

"You've been great—and you must have my aunt's special French toast. It's really the best!"

She went to get Davey, Suzie and Sean from their rooms.

Of everyone, Suzie was looking the worst for wear. Frazzled.

"I'm just hoping I have a job when we get out of all this," she said. Then she winced. "Of course, I'm hoping to have a life first, and then a job."

Sean was dealing with it better. "I'm seeing it as a very strange vacation. She's usually too tired for sex!" he whispered to Sarah.

"Sean!"

"I'm trying to get a lot of sex in!"

"Sean!" Suzie repeated in horror.

"Oh, come on…hey, I'll bet you Sarah is getting a little, too!"

"French toast, at the moment!" Sarah said. She turned to head out; Suzie and Sean followed her.

They gathered around the table. Special Agent Lawrence said they were free to address her by her first name—Winona. She was a ten-year vet with the force, they learned as they passed eggs, French toast and bacon around the table.

"Agent Parton—Cody—is a newbie, really. He's been with us about a year and a half. Thankfully, there's a constant stream of recruits. It's a busy world, you know."

So it seemed, Sarah thought.

"Tell me about your books," Winona Lawrence said, looking at her. "I admit to being a sci-fi geek!"

"She's working on alien bugs now!" Davey said excitedly.

He explained. Sarah was glad he was doing the talking when her phone rang. It was Tyler.

"You okay?"

"Everything is good here," she said. And she added, "The agents are great."

"Some are more personable than others, so Craig has told me. That makes them good at different things. Anyway, I'll be a while. I wanted to make sure you were okay. We've found out Perry Knowlton has most probably dressed as a woman often. We have a list of his most recent purchases."

"But you weren't able to find him?"

"No." He hesitated. "There's some kind of a new lead. We don't really know what. Craig's director just called and asked him to come in. We have the image of Knowlton's latest appearance out with a number of patrol officers. They're still looking. I'll call back in when I know more."

"Okay, great. I'm fine here," Sarah assured him.

She hung up. Conversation had stopped. Everyone was looking at her.

"We're getting close, I believe!"

There was silence.

Then Special Agent Lawrence said, "Well! I can't wait to read your latest novel, Sarah! You have a wonderful fan club here."

Sarah smiled. And wished she could remember what they'd been talking about before Tyler's call.

She couldn't.

It didn't matter. She realized it was going to be a very long afternoon.

"Director Egan didn't mention what arrived?" Tyler asked Craig.

"I just got a message from his assistant—come in as soon as possible," Craig said.

Tyler thought he could have stayed on the streets, searching, but he didn't think Knowlton was going to allow himself to be found that easily.

He was out there, though. And he was a chameleon. That made the situation even more frightening than before.

He'd made the decision to come with Craig. The FBI just might have something that could lead them to Perry Knowlton. The man had no known address. According to all official records, he didn't exist. He'd died a decade ago.

But he was breathing and in the flesh—and killing people—whether he was dead on record or not.

They reached the FBI offices and went through the security check required by everyone, agents included, and then headed up to the director's office. Egan's assistant sent them in.

Egan was on the phone, but he hung up, seeing that they'd arrived.

"We've had a message from the killer," he said. "It literally arrived ten minutes ago."

"We've received hundreds of messages from hundreds of 'killers,'" Craig said wearily. He looked at Tyler. "You'd be amazed by the number of people who want to say they're killers, or to confess to crimes they didn't commit."

"I think this one is real," Egan said. He glanced at Tyler. "It was actually addressed to you, as well as this office."

"And?" Tyler said.

"Apparently, Perry Knowlton wants to be a poet, too," Egan said. He tapped a paper that lay on his desk and slipped on his reading glasses. "Don't worry—this is a copy. The real deal is with forensics. Anyway, 'Six little children, perfect and dear, wanting the scare of their lives. One little boy, smarter than the rest, apparently felt like the hives. They went into the house, they cried there was a louse, and one fine man was gone. But now they pay the price today... six little children. One of them dead. Soon the rest will be covered in red.'"

"Six little children. Well, we weren't exactly little, but in a way, we were still children," Tyler said. "But he makes no mention of having killed the wrong Suzie Cornwall."

"He might not want to admit that he made a mistake," Craig said.

"Sounds like it might be legit," Egan said. "Naturally, we're testing everything, finding out about the paper and the typeface and all...and what came with it."

"What came with it?" Tyler asked.

"A C-1, I understand," Egan said. "According to doctors, there are seven cervical spine bones in a human being. The C-1 vertebra is closest to the skull. We received one—and we believe it might well have belonged to Hannah Levine. When a victim has been beheaded, the neck bones may well be crushed or… We're comparing DNA. But I do believe that we'll discover it belonged to Hannah."

"So now he's taunting the police. But we just put the images of Perry Knowlton out today—how did he know so quickly that we know who he is?" Craig wondered aloud.

"This arrived via bike messenger. I've emailed you the address for the service. I'll need you to look into it. You should get going," Egan said.

"Yes, sir. We need to inform Detective Green…" Craig said.

"Already done," Egan assured him.

They left the office.

THE MESSENGER SERVICE'S office was just north of Trinity Church, on Cedar Street.

The clerk behind the desk was pale. He was young and uncertain, with a pockmarked face and shaggy brown hair. "I know… I talked to a man from the FBI. I…I have a log, of course. I—I, oh, God! He didn't really say anything—just that the FBI had to know about a package! Was it a bomb? Did we handle a bomb?"

"It wasn't a bomb," Craig said. "What we need to know is who gave you the package to deliver?"

"Um…" The clerk fumbled with a roster on the

counter. "Jacob Marley. He paid cash. It was a man...
an old man, hunched over, crackling voice. Told me he
didn't believe in those newfangled credit card things.
He believed in cold, hard cash."

The clerk looked up at them. "Um, we still take
cash."

"You're the one who received the package here?"
Tyler asked.

"Yes, sir. Er, I should really see your credentials."

Craig flipped out his badge. The clerk swallowed
hard.

"It was a transaction like dozens of others. People
do still use cash. I mean every day, people use cash!"

"Did you notice where the man went?" Craig
asked. "Or where he came from?"

The clerk shook his head. "It was a busy morning.
But...there's a subway station just down the street."
He tried to smile. "Don't think he'd use a newfangled
thing like a car, huh? Then again...I don't know. But
he didn't look like the kind of guy who'd be driving
a car around the city. How old is the subway?" he
wondered.

"Built in 1904," Tyler said briefly, wondering how
he remembered the exact year. He'd actually seen a
documentary on it, he recalled, and then impatiently
pushed the history lesson aside. "But he was here not
long ago, right?"

"About an hour ago...yeah!" He suddenly seemed
proud of himself. "I have it on the roster!"

Craig started to say more; Tyler touched him on
the shoulder.

"The subway," Tyler murmured. "There's no other way. He was just up by the theater district, and while we were going crazy running around and checking out the clothing store, he was on the subway headed here, changing his appearance. He left the package. And then he—then, hell, he went back to wherever it is he comes from."

"He's been in New York City a long time," Craig mused. "He knows the system."

"I'll bet that he more than knows it. Craig, long shot here, but he's had plenty of time to study it. I was watching a program on the roots of the subway and the progression through the years. We know he can leap quickly and know where he's going." Tyler paused and took a deep breath. "Long shot, like I said. I can't help but think that he really knows the subway and the history of it—knows it like the back of his hand. There are so many abandoned stations. We know that the homeless often find them in winter. Do you think it's possible he's living underground somewhere?"

Craig listened and then nodded slowly. "Underground New York. We just had a case that involved the deconsecrated church right behind Finnegan's. Yeah, the subway."

"We know that people do make use of the empty space—warm, and out of snow and sleet and all in winter. An abandoned station—that might even be lost to the history books?" Tyler suggested.

"Surely, in ten years, the man has needed to bathe.

Needed running water. A way to eat and drink and sleep and—survive," Craig said.

Tyler shrugged. "I know I'm speculating, but it does work. Okay. My mom told me that once, when I was a kid and we were traveling on vacation, we wound up in Gettysburg and couldn't get a hotel room. So she and my dad parked the car in the lot of a big chain hotel—so we could slip in and use the bathrooms in the morning. Maybe our guy is doing the same thing. Not from a parking lot, but an abandoned station somewhere near several hotels…places he could slip in to use the facilities. Maybe hotels with gyms that have showers—he's evidently good at changing his image constantly. Wouldn't be hard for such a con to snatch a key and learn the identity of a paying guest."

"Possible," Craig said. "Hey, we went on theory. Theory has proved true. We'll head back to the office. In fact…" He pulled out his phone. "Mike should be in. I'll have him get started, pulling up all the spec sheets we'll need."

"Sounds good," Tyler said, and then he was quiet.

"What?" Craig asked, clicking off after speaking with his partner.

"That poem…it still bothers me."

"Because it was bad? Because it mentioned Davey and Sarah and the others?"

Tyler shook his head. "Because it didn't mention the Suzie Cornwall who is dead. He said 'one.' Made it sound as if he just killed one."

"Maybe he doesn't consider a mistake to be one of his kills."

"Maybe. Still…" Tyler shrugged. "You know, I can't help but want this bastard dead. By the same token, I want him alive. I want him answering questions."

"Well, we have to find him if we're going to take him in," Craig said pragmatically, "dead or alive."

SARAH WAS RESTLESS and didn't want to stay at the safe house any longer.

She wanted to be doing something.

Of course, she knew she'd be stupid to head out.

She did the dishes and played a Guess the Hollywood Star game with Davey—knowing full well he'd beat her soundly, and fairly.

Then Tyler called to bring her up to date—it seemed Perry Knowlton had sent a message and a bone to the FBI offices, taunting them.

She was glad when Kieran arrived with her brother Kevin. Due to Kieran's connections, she and Kevin had been given special dispensation to visit.

They sat together in one of the little chair groupings in the living room area. Craig, of course, had informed Kieran what was going on, and she and Kevin had come to tell Sarah about one of the recent cases they had wound up working on—or rather, that Craig had worked on, and which had involved them. It had revolved around the deconsecrated church and a killer who'd left his victims "perfect" in death.

"The point is, he liked the underground." Kieran paused and looked at her brother. "He killed a young actress Kevin had been seeing."

"I'm lucky I was never charged with the murder," he said grimly.

"I think they're right. I think it's the only solution. This guy has been hiding underground and taking advantage of his obsession with dressing up and—so it seems—his ability to borrow other identities," Kieran said.

"It makes sense." Sarah added, "Tyler said they were going to find a place near hotels—somewhere he could use facilities when he needed them. He's probably a very adept thief—the kind who steals small-time and therefore is never apprehended."

"Quite possibly. Anyway, we think they're on the right track," Kieran said.

Tyler called again then. Sarah hastily told Kieran and Kevin it was him.

"They're at an abandoned station not far from here," she said when she'd hung up. "But so far nothing."

"They'll keep looking," Kieran assured her. "People have the images and they know."

Next, Craig called Kieran. Sarah saw her wince.

"What?" she asked when Kieran clicked off.

"Well, they're getting calls and leads," she said.

"That's good, right?"

"Yes, except it's hard to winnow through them. Apparently, someone even called in about Craig and

Tyler. They're phoning in about every man over six feet in the city of New York!"

"Oh!" Sarah said.

"Don't worry, they'll keep working."

Davey peeked his head out. "Want to play a game?" he asked.

"Davey," Sarah murmured uncomfortably. "They're probably busy..."

"We'd love to play a game!" Kieran said.

And so they all played.

For once, Sarah won.

Davey was her teammate.

THE DAY WAS long and hard.

When eight o'clock came around, Tyler and Craig decided to wrap it up and start again in the morning.

They didn't want to be obvious about what they were doing; they didn't want Perry Knowlton to know they were actively searching underground for him.

They'd been provided with a really good map of the defunct stations—those that had existed years ago and were not in use now.

They needed more, Tyler thought. More to go on.

But shortly after eight, they returned to the safe house.

Sarah looked at Tyler anxiously. So did the others.

"We'll be starting up again in the morning," he assured them all. "We did take a step forward today. Another step tomorrow. We will catch the bastard."

He once again tried to get Sarah to stay at the safe house.

She absolutely refused.

He was, on the one hand, very glad.

Because there was nothing like getting back to the hotel room with her. There was nothing like apologizing, telling her he'd been underground, digging around in tunnels.

And then having her join him in the shower. Hot water sluicing over her breasts, her naked body next to his...

Touching, caressing.

Feeling her make love to him in return.

Falling hot and wet and breathless on the clean sheets in the cool air...

Being together, laughing, talking, not talking, being breathless...

Feeling the release of a tremendous climax.

And lying next to her as the little tremors of aftermath swept through him, allowing a sweet relief and tremendous satiation.

He loved her.

He always would.

And she loved him, too.

He just wondered if being so much in love could be enough.

Love was supposed to conquer all. But not if she pushed him away.

He'd think about that later.

The day had been long, but the night could be very sweet.

He allowed his fingers to play over the curve of her

back, caress the soft, sleek flesh and then fall lower again, teasing…

She let out a soft, sweet sigh.

"What are you thinking?" he asked her quietly.

"I'm not thinking," she said.

He didn't press it. He just held her. And they lay silently together once again.

A bit later, she moved against him. She teased along his spine with her tongue. Her fingertips were like a breath over his flesh. Her arms wound around him, and he curled toward her and she continued to tease and play and seduce.

They made love again.

And then held one another.

He should have had nightmares. He did not. He slept deeply, sweetly.

And then his alarm went off.

It was morning again. Perry Knowlton was still out there.

And God alone might guess what he would do next.

Chapter Eight

"I wish I could go with you," Sarah told Tyler.

He hesitated. They were showered and dressed, ready to leave.

"I can be helpful—hey, the bartender at Time and Time Again liked me better than you."

He had to smile at that. "Yeah, so...most guys out there are going to like you better than me. And, yes, you have proved helpful."

He wasn't lying. She had been very useful. That didn't change the fact that her being in danger could compromise his—or Craig's—ability to work.

"You're just better at the safe house!" he told her gently.

"Time goes so slowly," she said. She brightened. "But actually, there were a few minutes yesterday when I almost had fun. Kieran and Kevin were by— we played one of Davey's games with him. It was great. Kevin acted out half of his clues for Kieran. We were laughing. I was so surprised they were willing to play."

"Why?"

"Well, they're busy, of course. They don't really have time to play Davey's games."

He was silent. There it was. Her insistence that only she could really be happy to play a silly game with Davey.

"What?" she murmured, sensing the change in him.

"You can be really full of yourself, you know."

She frowned, stepping away. "What?"

"Never mind. Let me get you to the safe house."

He stepped out; she followed, still frowning. "Tyler?"

"Let's go."

He got her out of the room and down to the car. Once they were in traffic, however, she pressed the point.

"What are you talking about?"

"Never mind. Now isn't the time to worry about it."

"When should I worry about it? When we're either dead or you're back in Boston?"

He stayed silent; traffic was heavy. She waited. When they reached the area of the safe house, she pushed again.

"Tyler, tell me what you're talking about."

"Davey," he said simply. "Who do you think you are, really? Other people like Davey, love Davey, and enjoy his company."

"I—I…" Sarah stuttered.

He saw one of the agents—Special Agent Lawrence—in front of the building. She waved at him, hurrying around to the driver's side of the car. "I'll take it for you—you can see Sarah safely up. It will be there…" She pointed to a garage entrance down the street. "Agent Frasier will be by for you in about ten minutes."

"Okay, thanks," Tyler said, getting out of the car. He walked around, but Sarah was already out and walking in ahead of him.

The agent at the desk nodded to them.

Sarah was moving fast; she got into the elevator first. He had to put his arm out to keep the door open.

He stepped in. She was staring straight ahead. He wasn't sure if she was furious or in shock.

"I told you it wasn't really the time."

She didn't reply. The elevator door opened on their floor. She hurried ahead. At the door she stopped and turned and looked at him. "You're not being fair! Davey is like love personified. He doesn't have a mean bone in his body. Of course people…most people…love him!"

"Then let him enjoy them without you feeling you need to be a buffer."

"I—I don't!"

"You do. You push everyone away."

The door opened. Special Agent Preston was there. "Hey. Did you see Winona? She went down to take the car."

"Yes, we met her."

"Craig is on his way."

"I'm going right down," Tyler said.

Sarah was still staring at him. Now she looked

really confused. And worried. Maybe she hadn't realized how overprotective she was—and how much
she had doubted other people. Him.

"Go in!" he told her.

He started back toward the elevator. Sarah gasped
suddenly, and he spun around—ready to draw on Special Agent Preston.

But the FBI agent just looked puzzled. And Sarah
was suddenly running toward him. "Tyler!"

"Sarah, we can talk later," he said softly.

"No, no, no! Nothing to do with us...with Davey.
The poem—the poem Perry Knowlton wrote. It was
about Hannah, right—not Suzie Cornwall."

"It seemed to be about Hannah." He paused,
frowning, wondering what she was thinking.

He'd memorized the poem, and spoke softly, re-
peating the words. "'Six little children, perfect and
dear, wanting the scare of their lives. One little boy,
smarter than the rest, apparently felt like the hives.
They went into the house, they cried there was a
louse, and one fine man was gone. But now they pay
the price today...six little children. One of them dead.
Soon the rest will be covered in red.'"

"Hannah. We know—from Luke, the bartender—
that Perry Knowlton hung around the bar near
Times Square. And he went to a dress shop there
semiregularly... He seemed to watch Hannah easily
enough. Maybe he ran into her by chance one time.
He was able to become a woman quickly. And then
get to the subway to gather and then deliver the pack-

age. Tyler, you need to be looking for something underground not far from the bar and the shop."

He smiled at her slowly. "That would make sense. You've got it, I think. Although…"

"What?"

"I didn't really see anything in that area. He was a regular at the bar, yes, so we looked, but… We'll have to look again."

"But you will look?" Sarah asked.

"Yes, of course."

He gave her a little salute. Then he continued on to the elevator.

"I WONDER WHAT we're costing the taxpayers," Suzie said dismally. She had just flicked the television off. They had seen the artist's sketch of Perry Knowlton one time too many.

Along with pictures of Suzie Cornwall.

The young woman had been ill, and the artist's rendering had allowed that to show.

But Suzie had turned white every time a picture of her came across the screen.

Sarah leaned forward. "Suzie, stop blaming yourself. He's killed before. If we don't get him now, he'll kill again."

Special Agent Lawrence heard them talking and came forward, just a bit hesitantly. "Please! I know you won't stop, but you have to try to. It's not your fault, Suzie. It's not your parents' fault for naming you, or your dad for having that surname. It's the fault of a sick and pathetic and deplorable criminal mind. You have to accept that. If you don't, you will make yourself crazy."

"If I live to go crazy," Suzie muttered.

"You will live," Winona said, solid determination in her voice. She smiled, and then shrugged, sighing. "Okay, maybe I look a little worn, because I am. I need some sleep. But don't worry. We have replacements coming. Hey, Parton, who is coming on next?" she called.

Cody Parton was at the desk by the door. "Guzman and Walsh, so I've been told," he called.

"Ah, Walsh is a new guy. Guzman has been around forever and knows the ropes. Trust me, you'll be safe!" she said.

She smiled and walked away.

"People can say anything. I can even know it's true. But I can't help it. If that young woman's name hadn't been Suzie Cornwall, she'd be alive now," Suzie told Sarah softly.

"Maybe something worse was in store for her," Sarah said.

Suzie shrugged. "I wish I could think of something productive to do. It hasn't been that long, but I feel as if we've been cooped up forever."

Sean poked his head out of their bedroom. "Hey, guys, wanna watch a movie?" He shrugged. "They have all the movies we could possibly want. Reciprocation…or the cable company sucking up to the Feds, not sure which!"

"I guess so," Suzie said. "A comedy! Sarah, you coming?"

Sarah smiled. "No, I think I'll sit here and...plot."

"Alien bugs, huh? You're going to sit there and go crazy thinking," Suzie said.

Sarah offered her a weak smile. "Am I overprotective of Davey?" she asked.

Suzie hesitated. "Oh, Sarah! Sad to say, I haven't been around you that much lately, so I don't know if you are or not."

"Did I...in high school, was I overprotective?"

"Yes. Sometimes you had the right to be. We weren't cruel kids, but we could be careless. But..."

"But?"

"You really didn't have to be with Tyler and me. And others, of course. Davey has to make a few mistakes on his own, but he's smart. He can handle it. Your uncle did teach him to watch out for the bad guys."

Suzie grimaced and went on into the room with Sean. Sarah sighed, sitting there, torn between thinking about her own mistakes and the fact that they were hunting for a killer.

"You doing okay?" Winona walked back over to her.

She nodded. "Fine, thanks. It just seems...seems like this is taking a very long time."

"This? Long? I was with the Organized Crime Unit for a while—oh, my God! We gathered info for months and months and...um, but this is different."

Sarah smiled.

It wasn't all that different.

It could take time. A lot of time.

"I'm going off in a bit. Can you think of anything I can do for you?" Winona asked.

Sarah liked the woman, really liked her. She smiled and shook her head.

"When do we see you again?"

"Two days. I'll be back on for the next three after that, twelve hours a day!"

"No offense, but I hope we're not here that long. Though you've been very nice."

Winona smiled. "You guys have been easy. I think your aunt and Davey are watching a movie, too. I'll check on everyone before I leave. The new agents are due here soon. Fresh agents. You know what I mean! Replacements!"

Sarah nodded and let her go, leaning back. She closed her eyes, wishing she could sleep, wishing Tyler was there, wishing...

Just wishing that she wasn't so tense, and so alone, wondering if she had pushed people away...

If only she hadn't been so young, so afraid and so unsure. Unable to believe not only in Davey, but in herself.

THEY WERE BELOW the giant high-rises, great pillars of concrete, stone and steel that rose into the sky.

Once upon a time, the subway stop had been called the South Playwright Station. Back then, there had been no movies, and the station had actually been part of the Interborough Rapid Transit Company—one of the predecessors of the modern system.

In those days, the theater district had reigned supreme—there had been no movies. There had not been giant IMAX screens, 3-D, tablets, notepads, computers or any other such devices.

People had flocked here as one of the theater stations. Then a part of the subway had collapsed, and it had been closed off.

One of the city's engineers accompanied Craig and Tyler down to the station. The access was tricky; they had to bend over and crawl half of it. Broken brick lay with beautiful old tile; the station name was still mostly visible, all in tile that was now covered with the dust of decades that had passed without the station being used. The walls were covered in colorful but menacing graffiti from intrepid urban explorers and vandals. Tracks were intermittent, here and there.

The three men used high-powered flashlights as they went, moving cautiously.

"I don't know," Tyler murmured. "This seems a likely location, but how the hell could a tall man come and go, in all manner and mode of dress?"

"There could be another access," the engineer told them. "One that isn't on the maps. I did some digging. I believe there were a few entries in some of the old buildings—in the foyers or on the corners."

"Maybe," Craig said. "I don't think there's anything here, though."

"Wait, let's not head up yet. I think...there's something ahead," Tyler said.

"A door off to the side?" Craig murmured.

There was a door ahead, they discovered. An old maintenance door.

The three of them quickened their pace.

THE NEW CREW was coming on.

Agent Winona Lawrence impulsively gave Sarah a hug. "We really should move like professional machinery, but…come on, I want you to meet the new guys. One of them I've never met—the guy we were expecting called in sick. Oh, and you're going to have another female agent coming in tomorrow. Her name is Lucinda Rivera. She's super. You'll like her, too. But for now…"

The new agents were at the door. Guzman was older—maybe fifty. He had graying hair and heavy jowls, but a good smile when he met Sarah.

The other agent was younger—forty or forty-five, tall, with close-cropped dark hair, a large nose and dark eyes. She wondered if she had met him before, maybe with Kieran and Craig.

"Walsh called in sick," he told them. "I'm Adler. Jimmy Adler. Nice to meet you, Sarah."

"All right, then. We're out of here. Sleep!" Lawrence said.

"A beer!" Parton admitted.

"Parton," Guzman said softly.

"Hey…"

Sarah laughed. "Enjoy your beer, Special Agent Parton."

He grinned. "Just say 'Goodbye, Cody!'"

"Goodbye, Cody!" she repeated.

Guzman took up a position by the door after locking it. "You can take the desk," he told Alder.

"Sure thing." The other agent complied.

They weren't going to be as friendly or as easygoing as Lawrence and Parton, Sarah decided. She went back to her chair in the little living room grouping. There were magazines on a table by the sofa. She picked up a *National Geographic* and started leafing through it. There was an article about a new discovery of underground tombs and mummies in the Sahara Desert. She tried to concentrate on the piece, loving the concept of extraterrestrials possibly creating some of the great works in Ancient Egypt. Aliens arriving on Earth thousands of years ago could lead to some great sci-fi ideas.

The agents were making occasional small talk with each other, but Sarah wasn't paying attention. She could block them out. Well, she could tell herself she was concentrating all she wanted.

All she could really do was sit tensely, wishing that Tyler would call.

She had been there awhile when she heard one of the doors click open slightly, and she looked up; Suzie was at her bedroom door, looking troubled.

Sean was right behind her. He beckoned to Sarah.

She went to the door and started to speak, but Sean caught her arm and whisked her in. "You have to talk Suzie down. She's having daydreams, nightmares."

"You weren't there!" she whispered to Sarah.

"I'm confused. I wasn't where?"

"You weren't with us when we first went into Cemetery Mansion. He talked to me…he talked. The thing in the room…the thing we think now might have been Perry Knowlton. He beckoned to me. He spoke… I told myself he was a robot, an automaton, whatever. I was so scared…"

"She's dreaming that she hears his voice," Sean said.

Sarah wasn't sure what, but something suddenly went off inside her.

Instinct?

Like an alarm bell louder than could be imagined.

"We've got to get out," she said. "Now. And fast. Move—move toward that dumbwaiter-slash-elevator they showed us on the first day. Move now. Fast, and silently. I'm getting Davey and my aunt Renee. Go. Go now."

They'd been expecting Agent Walsh.

Walsh had "called in sick."

Maybe she was crazy—maybe she and Suzie were both cabin-crazy, paranoid—justly so, but paranoid.

Maybe.

But maybe not.

THEY MOVED AS quickly as they dared over the rubble and through the dust they raised, to the door at the side of the tunnel.

"Careful," the engineer warned. "You guys want to make it, to keep on searching, right?" he asked cheerfully. "Of course, we could do this for days!"

"Let's hope not," Craig said.

The engineer shrugged. "It's okay by me. I like you guys!"

"Thanks," Tyler said.

Maybe they *were* wrong.

And maybe they were right, but they weren't looking in the right place. Besides tunnels, as Kieran had pointed out to Sarah, streets had been built on top of streets in New York City. Not to mention—as the Finnegan family had all known from a previous case—there were underground tombs scattered about, as well.

But logically, Tyler didn't think Perry Knowlton had been living in a tomb. Unless there was such a thing with easy access to the city streets.

Yet even as they reached the door, he couldn't help but remember the poem Knowlton had written and sent to the police with a bit of neck bone.

Six little children, perfect and dear, wanting the scare of their lives. One little boy, smarter than the rest, apparently felt like the hives. They went into the house, they cried there was a louse, and one fine man was gone. But now they pay the price today... six little children. One of them dead. Soon the rest will be covered in red.

He hadn't realized he'd spoken aloud. Craig stopped walking; Tyler nearly plowed into him.

"Poem still bothering you?" Craig asked. The engineer walked ahead of them.

"I don't know—I just think he would want to

gloat over having killed two women so viciously," Tyler said.

"He is in revenge mode."

"Yes. Still, wouldn't he taunt us by saying, hey, and look what I did while I was trying to get the right people?"

"We need to catch him. Then we'll know."

"Wow, this is weird!" the engineer called back to them.

"What's that?"

"Door opens easy as if it had been greased yesterday!" And then he added a horrified "Holy crap!"

Tyler ran forward, Craig right with him.

The door opened to a little room lit by an electric lantern—a very modern electric lantern. There were boxes everywhere, an ice chest, Sterno…a mattress, pillows, blankets.

And in the middle of the floor, a man.

Stripped down to his underwear.

Blood streaked across his temple from a gaping head wound.

Craig was instantly down by his side. "Walsh, just met him the other day. He's got a pulse, slight… I'm pretty sure he was left for dead… His suit is…gone."

"You, sir! Stay with this man," Craig said. He was already trying his cell—and swearing when there was no signal.

"We've got to get to the safe house, have to send a warning. We have to get there!" Tyler said.

He wasn't sure he'd ever felt such a cold and deadly fear.

He was ready to rush back and crawl through the opening, ready to run all the way down Broadway. He was desperate to reach Sarah.

"There!" the engineer cried. "There's your entrance!"

And there it was. Across the little room was another door. Tyler rushed to it and threw it open. Stairs led up, and he took them to another door, then a hallway that twisted and turned.

At the end of the next hallway was a door that led to the foyer of a 1930s building. He burst out of it, with Craig behind him. He heard Craig dialing 9-1-1 for the man in the tunnel.

Tyler tried Sarah's number.

There was no answer.

DAVEY WAS PAYING ATTENTION. He wasn't watching his movie; he was at the door, ready when Sarah slipped across the hall as quietly as possible to open it. He brought a finger to his lips.

"What is it?" Renee asked.

"Shh, shh, shh, Davey is right!" Sarah told her. "Come with me. We have to get out of here."

"Get out of here?" Renee said, puzzled. "But we have FBI guards—"

"I think they've been compromised. If I'm wrong... we'll come right back up. But we're going to take the emergency exit. We have to get to the elevator—the escape dumbwaiter we were shown."

"Sarah, what has happened?"

"Nothing—yet. But please believe me—"

"I have my Martian Gamma Sword!" Davey said. And he did. He produced it, showing them that he was ready to fight.

"Please, I could be wrong, but if not, hurrying may be essential. Please, Aunt Renee!"

Renee still didn't appear to be happy. She looked out the door, down the hall to the living area.

Guzman and Adler seemed to be doing their jobs.

"Please!" Sarah said.

"Mom. Come!" Davey said. He looked at Sarah and said, "You know my mom. Really, sometimes she's a little Down syndróme, too. She concentrates, and you have to shake her up. You know that."

"Now!" Sarah said firmly.

She took her aunt's hand and led the way out. Renee grabbed Davey's arm. They headed silently out of the room and down the hall toward the little enclave where the dumbwaiter/elevator waited.

Of course, they'd never tried it.

Aunt Renee whispered that concern. "What if it doesn't work? What if five of us don't fit? What if the agents are furious?"

She'd barely voiced the question before they heard a thump.

Sarah stared back toward the door to the apartment.

Adler was standing over Guzman.

He still held the muzzle of an FBI Glock in his hand; he'd used the handle to cream the agent on the head.

"Go!" Sarah screamed as the man turned to look at them.

They ran.

"Hurry!" Sean beckoned from inside the elevator.

Sarah was still looking back as she ran. The others plowed into the elevator.

She stared right at the man. The thing. The monster the others had seen that night long ago—but she and Davey had not.

Because he'd already been out of the haunted house. Maybe he'd known that his fellow murderer was on a suicidal spree.

Now he looked right at her.

And he smiled.

He aimed the gun at her.

"Sarah!" Davey shouted.

She jumped into the contraption; they were on top of one another, like rats.

Sean hit the giant red Close Door button.

A shot went off.

The door shut just in time.

They heard the bullet strike...

"His voice! Oh, God, I knew that voice!" Suzie sobbed.

Yes! Thank God she had!

The elevator sped toward the ground floor, and Sarah prayed they could get out and get free and find help...

He didn't have just a knife anymore. Maybe, recently, he'd had a gun along with him as well for his murders. Maybe that was how he'd forced his victims to their murder sites.

Maybe...

"Oh, God, he's coming for us all!" Suzie cried.

ALL THE OFFICIAL cars and all the official power in the world couldn't really move New York City traffic.

Up and out of the tunnel, Tyler and Craig didn't even try it.

On the street level, Craig was able to reach Dispatch to request help; officers would be on the way.

But so would they—via the subway.

Miraculously, they were able to hit an express.

And off the subway, they ran.

Bursting into the foyer of the safe house, Tyler stopped at last.

The desk clerk was on his feet, hurrying toward them. "Agents are up there," he said. "Guzman was down. That man came in with Guzman...he had credentials. There was no reason to suspect... He walked right in. Right by me and the backup. I'm here, but everyone else is out there, on the street. We have people going through the rooms, but..."

"But what?" Tyler roared. He realized that Craig had spoken at the same time.

"They got out, the witnesses... We don't know exactly where now—they didn't come this way. They sensed something was wrong somehow, but...they're out on the street. We have men out there, but—"

Tyler didn't give a damn just how many men might be out on the street. He turned, followed by Craig.

"Hey!" the agent called to them. "Hey, this is important!"

Tyler barely paused.

"He's armed! He has a service Glock. He doesn't just have a knife—"

As the clerk spoke, they heard the explosive sound of a gun being fired.

SARAH HAD REMEMBERED the door would open only from their side—and only when she pushed the button.

She did so. They'd come out in an alley. If they didn't move quickly, they'd be trapped.

"Run! Go!" she commanded.

They tumbled out and began running. The good thing for them was the main door to the building was around the corner; Knowlton had to leave the building that way—his only choice. That gave them precious seconds to get out of the alley, get somewhere…hide!

She had Davey's hand. He was not the most agile person she knew; he wasn't necessarily fast when he ran. She was desperate to find a hiding place before they were seen.

"Davey!" Her aunt cried her son's name with anguish. Sarah knew that she hated being even one second away from him when there was danger.

She paused, but her aunt, panting, looked at her desperately. "Take him! Take him, keep him safe!"

Sarah nodded. She tightened her grip on his hand and ran on.

Luckily, the street was thronging with people. She kept screaming for help.

They moved out of the way.

Some pulled out cell phones—she hoped they were dialing 9-1-1.

Gasping for air, Sarah soon felt she was reaching her limit.

Trinity was ahead of her.

She had Davey; she had to pray Aunt Renee and Sean and Suzie would run faster than she could with Davey. They could truly get away, would find a shop, a restaurant, anything! Duck in...

She was on the street, ready to run into the Trinity graveyard, when she heard someone shouting at her. She turned.

It was a police officer in uniform.

She drew Davey behind her. "He's after us! The killer is after us—Knowlton, the man who beheaded the two women...he's after us!"

"Now, now, miss!" the officer said. "Miss, I'm not sure what your problem is, but you're just going to have to try to calm down."

"My problem is that a killer is after us!"

"Is this some kind of a crazy game?" the cop demanded.

"No, dammit! Sorry, sorry, Officer, please, I'm begging you—listen to me. There is a killer—"

She broke off. The man who had claimed to be

Special Agent Adler—and was, beyond a doubt, Perry Knowlton—was now casually strolling toward them.

"Get over the fence. Hide in the graves!" she whispered to Davey.

"I won't leave you!" Davey said stubbornly.

"Do it!" she snapped.

To her relief, for once, he obeyed her.

And it was all right; Knowlton was just staring at her. Smiling still.

"Special Agent Adler, Officer, FBI," Knowlton said, ever so briefly flashing a badge. "And that woman is a dangerous psychopath!"

"He's going to shoot me," she told the police officer calmly.

"No, no, miss. He's FBI. Now, I don't know the truth here, but he'll talk to you and—"

Knowlton took aim and fired.

Sarah gasped as the officer went down before her. He was screaming in agony.

Not dead.

Knowlton might be good with a knife—he wasn't that great with a gun.

Sarah was dimly aware of the sound of dozens of screams; people were shouting, running, clearing the street.

And then Knowlton was looking right at her. He was a few feet away from her.

His stolen gun was aimed at her.

"You don't want to shoot me," she told him quietly.

He paused and smiled, clearly amused.

"I don't?"

"You don't like guns. You use them only to scare and bully people—when you have to. This may be the first time you're really using one."

"Sorry—I used guns we stole off the guards when Archie and I escaped."

"Still, you're not very good with a gun. You're much more adept with a knife. And I'm assuming you have one. You like to torture your victims, and that's much better accomplished with a knife."

"Don't worry—I'm carrying a knife. And," he added softly, "when I finish with you, I will find that cousin of yours. Oh, I read the papers, I saw the news! He was the hero, huh? Let's see if he dies like a hero. Oh, dear! Look around. A graveyard. How fitting!"

He smiled. Whether he liked a gun or not, he still had the Glock aimed at her.

"Drop it!" she heard someone say.

She smiled with relief. Sanity! Someone who realized that Knowlton wasn't the law—that he was a killer.

Someone…

Her turn to know a voice.

"Drop it!"

Knowlton stared at her. Smiled. Took careful aim—and then spun around to shoot at whoever was behind him.

A gun went off.

For a moment, it felt as if time had been suspended. As if the world had frozen—it was all a special effect in a movie, because, dear Lord, this couldn't be real. The killer, there, posed before her…

And then he fell.

She looked past him, her knees wobbling, something inside her desperately fighting to keep her standing, to keep her from passing out.

There, past the prone body of Perry Knowlton, was Tyler.

She stared at him for a moment.

And then she ran, and he was ready to take her into his arms. She knew she wasn't shot; she wasn't sure about him.

"Tyler, Tyler…"

"I'm fine. I'm fine, I'm fine," he assured her, holding her, smoothing back her hair. "Are you…?"

"Fine. I'm fine. He aimed at you, Tyler, he aimed at you. He—"

"I'm okay. We're okay," he said firmly.

She was aware that Craig was with them then, briefly checking on the two of them, then hurrying forward to hunker down by the body of the fallen killer.

Others were moving in.

Davey had crawled back over the fence. He raced to them.

Tyler pulled him close, as well.

"Group hug!" Davey said.

Sarah drew back, looking anxiously at Tyler. "Aunt Renee, Suzie, Sean…?"

"They're all right. They went into a clothing store. They're good. We're all alive. All of us… Guzman and Walsh are being rushed to the hospital, and—"

Sirens suddenly screamed.

Chaos seemed to be erupting with a flow of agents and police, crime scene tape—a flurry of activity.

But none of it mattered.

She was being held in Tyler's arms. And anything could happen around her. They had survived again. And this time…

She wouldn't just survive. She would live.

Chapter Nine

Sarah and Kieran Finnegan helped serve the table.

The pub wasn't so terribly busy. It was Wednesday afternoon and the after-work crowd had yet to come in.

Sarah hadn't worked in the pub for years, but Kieran seemed to know that helping with the simple task of supplying wine, beers—regular and nonalcoholic—and a Shirley Temple for Davey was busywork, and sometimes it helped.

They should have all been more relaxed.

Knowlton had been dead now for several days. All the paperwork was done. There had been a dozen interviews with all manner of law enforcement, and then with major broadcasters and newspaper journalists. The Perry Knowlton story was still holding reign over the internet, TV, and papers and magazines everywhere.

That day, however, had not been about Perry Knowlton for Sarah and her friends.

That afternoon, they had gathered to bury Hannah Levine. There had been tears of sorrow and regret; friendship was a terrible thing to lose. And as they'd gathered at the grave after services, Sarah was pretty sure they were all looking back over the years and wondering how the killings at Cemetery Mansion had cost so many their lives—and left behind survivors who were emotionally crippled. There was no way out of wondering how they had let Hannah down. Each individual alive was responsible for his or her own life—they knew that. But they also knew human relationships were priceless and, for most, essential for living.

Sarah had been named as Hannah's next of kin. She arranged for a really beautiful nondenominational ceremony. Hannah's dad had been Jewish; her mom a Methodist, but Sarah wasn't sure Hannah had adhered to either religion. Or any.

But she had been left in charge. And Sarah wanted very much to believe in God and goodness and a higher power. She thought the service was not religious, but spiritual. She guessed Hannah would have liked it.

After the funeral and burial, they gathered at Finnegan's. And just as they had felt lost before, they were all trying to tie up the last little skeins of confusion in their own minds.

"I wonder… I mean, when you were trying to find Knowlton, find out if he could be alive…you found so many other victims. How will…how will you make all that go together?" Sean asked, sipping his beer.

"Agents in my office will do what they can to find out what happened where and when," Craig said.

"Most forensic work does take time. We were incredibly lucky—beyond lucky, considering Knowlton's sudden surge toward suicide in his determination to kill you all—that we did make the right calculations in following his movements."

"And we're lucky Sarah got us out!" Suzie said, lifting her glass of white wine to Sarah.

"You knew his voice. After ten years, you recognized his voice," she answered.

"And Davey was ready to move quickly!" Sean said.

"To Davey—our hero!" Tyler said.

They all lifted their glasses to Davey. He smiled and lifted his Shirley Temple. "To best friends forever!" he said, and then grinned. "And to Megan. I get to see my girlfriend tomorrow!"

Everyone laughed. He passed a picture of Megan around. They all assured him she was a pretty girl, and she was.

There was a stretch of silence around the table, and then Tyler spoke.

"I really wish we could have taken him alive," he said. "There was a lot we could have learned from him. I still want to know how the hell he broke in to the playground to be able to display the poor woman he killed, thinking she was our Suzie."

"I do, too," Craig said. "But since he was aiming at your heart, you had no choice but to fire. You know, he would have shot you—and then Sarah. And then he'd have gone for Davey and killed anyone else in his way—until he was stopped. Our agents are still in the hospital. Guzman might be out in a day or two. Luckily, Knowlton didn't really know how to kill someone with a knock on the head. Walsh—the fellow we found in the subway tunnel—will be another week or so. But his prognosis is good. Then there's the cop he shot on the street—he'll be in the hospital for a few weeks. Needs several surgeries. So, Tyler, yeah, you shot and killed him. You saved your own life—and probably others."

Sarah made a mental note to visit the agents and the police officer in the hospital. She hadn't done so yet.

"How did he find us?" Suzie wondered.

"He wasn't just good at hiding," Tyler said. "He excelled at being a people watcher. He was excellent at observation, something he learned—according to earlier notes we recently dug back up from the horror park murders—from the man he admired and all but worshipped, Archibald Lemming. The guards had said that Lemming loved to hold court—and Knowlton loved to listen and learn. Patience, Lemming had taught him, was a virtue. So Knowlton discovered the safe house—by lurking around in any number of his disguises and maybe by following one of us. He watched, and he found an agent he could take by surprise. He was adept at so many things, and he was able to bide his time and wait."

"And," Craig said, "we found out that he stole his 'Adler' FBI identification three years ago. The man did know how to wait and bide his time. He took Special Agent Walsh down for his plain blue suit—and to keep him from showing up at work. He called in sick on Walsh's phone, left him to die in the tunnel—after stealing his gun. Once you all escaped him and he was out on the street, I think he decided he'd kill until he was killed himself—but of course, we were the focus of the rage he's had brewing for the last decade."

They talked awhile longer; they enjoyed shepherd's pie.

Then Suzie and Sean prepared to leave, hugging everyone.

"We need to keep in touch this time," Suzie said. "I think...I think we're relieved and grateful—and sad. But..."

"But we will keep in touch—I've missed you, Suzie. Yes, we will be haunted by what happened to Hannah. But we'll stay friends this time. And I think it will help," Sarah assured her, hugging her tightly in return.

Sean shook hands with Tyler, then the two embraced. "Hey, Boston isn't that far, my friend. We have to all keep in touch," he said.

Tyler nodded. "Yes. Of course."

Sarah noted he didn't refute the fact that Boston wasn't far.

Her heart sank a little. He was returning to his old life; she would be returning to hers.

She thought of the nights they'd been together since Knowlton had died. They had been intense.

They hadn't talked yet. Not really talked. They had made plans for Hannah's funeral. They had answered any last-minute questions they could for the police and the FBI.

It had been easier just to be together.

Davey got up from the table. He was anxious to leave; Renee was taking him for a haircut so he could look his best when he saw Megan.

"I got a girlfriend!" he reminded them all.

Soon after, Tyler smiled at Sarah and asked her softly if she was ready to go.

She nodded.

They weren't staying at the hotel any longer. They went to her apartment on Reed Street.

When the door was closed, he pulled her into his arms and very tenderly kissed her lips.

And suddenly, all the things she wanted to say came tumbling out of her mouth. "I'm so sorry. I don't know why. I think I was always afraid...maybe I didn't want to be hurt myself, and so I tried to make sure Davey wasn't hurt. It seemed to be a way to cope. There are bad people out there...or sometimes, just rude and unkind people. I haven't been... I've been... I just knew how some people felt some of the time, and I love my aunt and Davey and my family, and...I...there was really no excuse. I never meant to push you away. I just didn't want others to feel they had to take on my responsibility—"

His finger fell on her lips. "Some people want part of your responsibility."

"Oh, I know that! And I should have had faith in

Davey being sweet and wonderful in his own right, I just…"

To her astonishment, Tyler slipped down to his knees. He looked up at her, eyes bright, and pulled a small box from his pocket. He flicked it open, offering it to her.

"Sarah, I've loved you forever. I've loved you when I was with you and when I wasn't with you. When I was away, you interfered with everything I would try to do, because I could never get you out of my memory…my heart, my soul. Sarah, we've wasted a decade of life, and life, as we all know, is precious. So…will you marry me?"

She was speechless, and then she fell to her knees in turn and began to kiss him. And they both started to shed their clothing, there on the hardwood at the entry to the apartment. When they were halfway stripped, he suddenly laughed, stood and pulled her up. "Let's not celebrate with bruises!" he said. She laughed, too, and she was in his arms again.

Making love had always been amazing. That afternoon…

Every touch, breath and intimacy seemed deeper, more sensual, more erotic. More climatic.

He stroked her back. Rolled and kissed her shoulder.

"Hmm. I think we celebrated. But you haven't actually said yes!"

"Yes! Yes…yes…"

She punctuated every yes with a kiss.

"I can go anywhere. I mean, we are New York-ers, but Boston is a great city," she said breathlessly. "I can and will go anywhere in the world with you. We can have a big wedding, we can elope, we can do anything at all. None of it matters to me, except being with you, waking up with you, going to sleep with you…" She stopped, then straddled him with a grin. "My Lord! I could write romance again. Giant bugs—and romance!"

He laughed. He pulled her to him, and they talked and talked, and made love again.

No big wedding. They weren't going to wait that long. A small ceremony at Finnegan's, applauded by whomever might be there, with just Kieran and Craig and Suzie and Sean—and, of course, their families, including—very especially—Davey and Aunt Renee.

Sometime that night, very late that night, they finally slept.

SARAH FELT THAT she was walking on air. She'd called Kieran, who was at work at the offices of Fuller and Miro, but she could meet for lunch.

Relief was an amazing thing. Or maybe it was happiness. So much time wasted, and yet maybe not wasted. She and Tyler had both grown through the years.

And now…

Now they were together. And she was going to marry him. It wasn't even that marriage mattered so much to her—that she would wake up every morning next to Tyler did. That wherever they went, whatever they did, she could go to sleep with him at night.

She'd loved him as long as she could remember.

And now...

The morning had been good. She had worked on her latest manuscript; an Egyptian connection, not through Mars, but through a distant planet much like Earth. The people had been advanced, kind and intelligent, and very much like human beings. A war with a nearby hostile planet had kept them away, and a shift in the galaxies had closed the wormhole they had used to reach Earth. But archeologist and mathematician Riley Maxwell had been with an expedition that had found a tablet, and the tablet had told them about the "newcomers," the "gods," who had come down from space and taught them building and water usage. Soon after her discovery, she was visited by a newcomer to their group, Hank McMillan, and he had been just as anxious to destroy all that she had discovered. And as they worked together and came under attack by a group with strange and devastating weapons, she'd begun to fall in love...all the while discovering Hank was an ancient alien, trying to close all the doors before the still hostile and warlike tribe arrived to devastate Earth...

Of course, they solved it all and lived happily ever after. Her outline was complete!

At eleven thirty, she left her apartment, smiling as she headed toward Broadway to walk down to Finnegan's.

Her steps were light.

She forgot all about the fact that New Yorkers supposedly didn't make eye contact.

She smiled and, yes, people smiled back.

It was a beautiful day, chilly, but with a bright sun high in the sky.

She was surprised when a police car pulled up by the corner ahead of her. She heard her name being called and, frowning, she hurried forward.

Happiness could be its own enemy. She was immediately afraid something had happened to Tyler. Or that something was wrong somewhere. Davey! Her aunt!

She rushed over to the car. Alex Morrison was at the wheel, and he was smiling.

"Hey, I'm glad I found you so easily!"

"You were looking for me? You could have called."

"Well, this just all came about. Hop in. I'll take you to Tyler."

"Oh. Is he all right?" she asked anxiously.

"He's fine, he's fine. We're working on putting some pieces together. With other events, you know?" he said somberly. "Anyway, come on, I'll get you to him and Craig."

"I have a lunch date with Kieran. I'll just give her a call."

"No need. We'll pick up Tyler and Craig and head to Finnegan's." He grimaced. "I can park anywhere with this car, you know."

"Sure. Okay." She walked around and slid into the passenger's seat and grinned at Alex. "You know, I've never ridden in a patrol car!" she said. "I'll give

Tyler a call and then let Kieran know that we might be a few minutes late."

"Oh, that won't be necessary!" he said, reaching over. She thought he was going for the radio.

He wasn't.

He made a sudden movement and backhanded her so hard that her head spun, then crashed into the door frame. Stars went reeling before her eyes.

Shadows and darkness descended over her, but she fought it.

Not now. Even as she felt her consciousness slipping away, she struck out.

"Damn you, tough girl, huh!"

Before he could hit her again, she scratched him. Hard. And as the darkness claimed her from his second blow, she knew that, at the very least, she'd drawn blood.

TYLER WAS BACK in Craig's office at the FBI. The Bureau's analysts had pulled up a number of murders, facts and figures, and they were still going over them. Victims had families. And, Tyler had discovered, not knowing what had happened to a loved one was torture for most families. "Closure" was almost a cliché. And yet it was something very real and necessary.

He was frowning when Craig asked him, "What? What now? There's something you don't like."

"There's something niggling me about that damned poem. I wanted to take Knowlton alive."

"Yeah, well, better that *you're* alive," Craig reminded him. "But…I do see what you mean. Knowlton claimed Hannah. She was dumped in the river."

"And Suzie Cornwall was left in a park."

"He could have been working on his methods. What he did wasn't easy—getting himself and a body over the fence. Setting the body up. The head—in a swing."

"Have they found any kin for her?" Tyler asked.

"No, but she had friends. Only, her friends didn't really seem to have much of anything. No one has offered a burial. Instead of the potter's field on this one, I thought the four of us might want to chip in quietly and bury her."

"Works for me," Tyler said.

He was quiet again. Then he quoted, "'But now they pay the price today…six little children. One of them dead. Soon the rest will be covered in red.'"

"I admit it bothers me, too."

"But I shot and killed him. So we'll never know."

"Is it possible for us to look through the photographs again?"

"Of course."

Craig left the office. Reports lay on the desk. Tyler started going over them again.

DNA.

The little vertebra Knowlton had sent to the FBI with his poem had proved to belong to Hannah Levine, not Suzie Cornwall.

That bothered Tyler as much as the poem. If the bone had just belonged to Suzie Cornwall…

He started reading the autopsy reports again. So much was so similar. Except...

Hannah had alcohol and drugs in her system. Suzie...

She'd had her medication. Dr. Langley believed her throat had been slit, prior to her head being removed.

Hannah...

Hard to tell, with the way her head and torso had been found, washed up from the river.

He drummed his fingers on the table. No usable forensics had been found at the park. It was almost as if whoever had done the crime had studied books on how the police found killers, on what little bits of blood and biological trace could give them away.

Craig walked back into his office. "I got what I could. I called over to Detective Green, asking if Morrison could make sure we had everything, but Alex Morrison called in sick today. He's not there to help me get everything, but at this point, I do think I have it all."

Tyler looked at Craig, listening to the words. And suddenly, he was up and on his feet, not even sure why, thoughts jumbling in his mind.

Alex Morrison had been at the theme park the night Archibald Lemming had killed so many in Cemetery Mansion.

He'd started out in the academy and had gone into forensics.

He knew what was going on with the police—and the FBI.

"We need to find him," Tyler said. "We need to find Alex Morrison."

SARAH CAME TO very slowly.

She wasn't at all sure of where she was. Somewhere deep and dank… It had a smell of mold and age and…earth.

She tried to move; she was tied up, she realized. Fixed to a chair. Her ankles were bound, her arms had been pulled behind her and her wrists secured.

Her head pounded. Her arms hurt. She ached all over. The world was horribly askew. She had to blink and blink.

Reality overwhelmed her. She was a prisoner. And it was perfectly clear. Knowlton hadn't committed all the murders. They had known something wasn't right. Alex Morrison had been a living, breathing, functioning psychopath all the time. So helpful! So helpful as he used everything they had learned, so helpful as he ever so subtly turned them toward Perry Knowlton.

A functioning psychopath? Maybe Kieran could explain such a thing…

She tried to move.

She realized she could struggle, but the best she could ever do would be tip the chair over.

Panic seized her. There was barely any light. She heard a strange droning sound, like a piece of machinery moving…

She grew accustomed to the dim light. Blinking, she saw that, ten feet from her, Alex Morrison was busy at some kind of a machine. She realized, nearly passing out again, it was some kind of a knife sharpener. Battery operated, certainly, but…

Did it matter how the hell it was operated? He

was sharpening his knife. To slit her throat, and then decapitate her.

This was where he had killed Suzie Cornwall. He'd made the mistake—not Knowlton. He'd killed her here, then he'd used a patrol car to dump her body. Easy enough. People seldom questioned a patrol car in a neighborhood, or an officer checking out a fence, or a park, or—

He turned.

"Ah, awake, I see! Oh, Sarah. I could have been nice and seen to it that I dispatched you before…well, you know. Before. But then again, your kind deserves to feel some pain!"

"My kind?"

She wished Kieran was with her. Kieran might know how to talk to such a man. A functioning psychopath.

But Kieran wasn't here. Sarah had to think as her friend might—as any desperate person might think! Think to talk, think to survive—until help could come!

But how and why would help come? No one knew where she was. Everyone thought all the danger was over. No one knew…

There was no chance of help!

And still she had to hang on. While there was breath, she had once heard, there was hope.

And everything suddenly lay before her. Tyler, their future life together that they had managed to deny one another years ago…

"What is my kind, Alex?" she asked again.

He looked at her, leaning against the shoddy portable picnic table that held his knife sharpener.

"Cheerleader!" he said.

"What?"

"Cheerleader. You know your kind!"

"Oh, my God, Alex. I haven't been a cheerleader in over a decade."

"You were a cheerleader then."

"When?"

"Oh, come on, Sarah, give me a break! That night…at Cemetery Mansion. You were a cheerleader. Oh, yes. You had your football-playing hunk with you and your retard cousin."

"Don't you dare use that word around me!"

"Whatever."

"Oh, you idiot! That's why people suffer so much in this life—that's the reason Tyler and I haven't been together. How dare you! Davey is an incredible human being. But I didn't believe Tyler really saw that—*because of people like you, you asshole!*"

She was startled to realize her rage had apparently touched him.

"Okay, okay, well, maybe you're right about Davey. I mean…from what I understand, it was somehow him who managed to bring about the fall of Archibald Lemming. A brilliant man like Lemming."

"A brilliant psychopath and killer, you mean. Not so brilliant, was he? He's dead. And Perry Knowlton, well, what an idiot!"

"Ah, but you aren't seeing *my* genius. Knowlton got sloppy. He got sloppy—because he was afraid I would strike again before he could. He wanted so badly to kill you all himself! Not to mention it was useful to me for everyone to suspect him. I overheard that bit about their stomach contents—steak. Oh, I loved it! What a cool clue to lead nowhere—the women just both liked steak. I wished that Tyler had gone a little crazier on the hunt for a steak house, but still! So gratifying. I did such a good job. I followed Knowlton, and I learned from watching. I learned my lessons well. And I was a step ahead."

"You're an ass. You killed the wrong Suzie Cornwall."

His eyes narrowed. "Well, I won't kill the wrong Sarah Hampton, will I?" he asked her.

"How did you get your victim over the fence?" she demanded.

He laughed. "Databases! I found a way to get a key. I opened the lock. I walked in with her leaned against me, like someone who needed assistance—maybe lost something like a cell phone, you know? I just looked like a city worker, a peon. It wasn't so hard. In fact, it was exciting. I had her body leaned against me, her head in a cooler, and I opened the lock and just walked on in. Then…fun. Setting her up. Locking the gates again. Exhilarating! It was great."

Sarah forced a smile. "They will know it's you. You've gotten away with a lot. Let me see…the night at Cemetery Mansion. You thought you wanted to be a cop—that would be a way to see murder and horrible things…and get paid for it! You were in forensics and you were called to the scene. And you saw exactly how gruesome all the blood and guts and gore could be."

"I admired Archibald Lemming to no end," he agreed. "Even as I took pictures of his cold, dead body."

"And you knew Perry Knowlton was still alive."

"I watched him leave the park."

"And you spent the next years trying to find him. Did you?"

"I did, about a month ago. But I never let on. I just watched. And after he killed Hannah...well, I thought I'd help him along. I have access to all kinds of information. I wanted to give him all the precious scoop I could get my hands on. Then maybe we could become partners. But hey...he ignored me. Ignored me! But now the police and your precious FBI friends are all patting themselves on the back. They think they're all in the clear. Well, I've got you—and before they find you, I'll have your darling Davey, too!"

"Davey is too smart for you," she said. "He was too smart for Archibald Lemming, and for Perry Knowlton—and he'll be too smart for you!"

Alex Morrison smiled. "You try to protect him— well, you would have. Too bad I didn't have you around...before. Oh, but you wouldn't have helped me. The cheerleaders laughed at me. The football players...well, I spent some time stuffed in a locker. Oh, and I had my head stuck in a toilet. And you know what my folks did when it happened? My mother put my head in the toilet, yelling at me to stand up. And my old man—you know what he did? He beat me with a belt—told me a man would handle himself. Well, I'm handling myself now. I'm ridding the world of cheerleaders and football players and popular people who stuff others in lockers. I mean, come on, seriously—they all need to go, right?"

"CAN IT BE this easy?" Craig asked.

Tyler wasn't thinking anything was easy. Sarah wouldn't answer her phone.

She was supposed to have met Kieran.

She hadn't.

Alex Morrison was nowhere to be found.

Craig hadn't tried to placate Tyler. He'd never suggested Sarah was all right somewhere, that she'd just forgotten her phone. That she was an adult and had just gotten busy.

There was no lie to believe in, and they hadn't tried to invent one. Time was everything; they didn't have much.

They had to find Sarah.

But Craig was right. They'd easily used the system to find the patrol car Morrison had been using.

And now they were using GPS on his phone.

Tyler was functioning. Get in the car, move, walk, use his mind...

Find Sarah, find Sarah...

But all the while, he was fighting terror again, that almost overwhelming terror he'd felt when they'd realized Perry Knowlton had taken down an FBI agent and was heading to the safe house.

Did Alex Morrison really believe he could get away with this? Would it matter, would anything matter, if he managed to kill Sarah?

"He's here, right on this spot," Craig said, frustrated. "We've got the old subway map, but I can't find anywhere that's an entry." He paused, looking around the street.

Tyler did the same; he stared at the map again. He scanned the buildings intently.

At the corner was an old stone apartment block. There was a grate, a vent from the massive subway system and underground city below.

It was New York. There were grates in sidewalks everywhere.

But the building appeared to have gone up in the early 1900s.

Right about the same time as the subway.

And the facade had never been changed.

He didn't speak; he rushed ahead of Craig and bent to pull on the grate. It seemed too tight. Craig reached past him, helping him twist the metal.

It gave.

There was a short leap down to an empty little room.

But as his eyes adjusted, Tyler saw an old wooden door.

And the door opened to a flight of ancient, worn stairs.

He and Craig looked at one another.

Tacitly silent, they started down.

At least Tyler prayed that he was silent. To him, his heart seemed to be beating loudly in an agonized staccato.

ALEX MORRISON CAME and hunkered down before Sarah, studying his well-honed knife and then looking at her with a satisfied smile.

"I guess I did want to torture you in a way. I mean, I spent days with my head in a toilet due to a cheerleader."

"I never did anything to anyone, Alex. I just liked cheerleading—I was good at gymnastics. And Tyler was never cruel to anyone in his life. He worked with a lot of the kids who weren't so good, on his own time. He got the coaches to have special days and special races... You're so wrong! Yes, people can be cruel. Kids can be cruel. We all know that, and to most of us, it's deplorable. I didn't have enough faith in people. But you...you're just a truly sad and pathetic case! Kill me. Do it. But it will never end what you feel. It won't help the hatred and rancor that fester constantly within you!"

As she finished speaking, she heard something.

She wasn't sure what.

Rats?

And then she saw. She didn't know how. It seemed impossible.

Tyler was there. Tyler and Craig. They had somehow known, had somehow found her...

Tyler made a motion to tell her to keep talking.

And she realized her position. Tyler was there, yes. And Craig. But Alex Morrison was in front of her. All but touching her. And he had his freshly honed, razor-sharp carving knife in his hands.

"You're wrong!" Alex was saying. "You're wrong. Every time I kill, I feel a little better. I feel I've sent one of you bitches or bastards on to a just reward!"

"You really should have gotten to spend a lot more time with Kieran Finnegan. She's a psychologist, not a psychiatrist—though her bosses are psychiatrists. She could explain to you that no, you were never going to feel better. I don't really get all of it—I majored in English and mass communication—but there are sociopaths and there are psychopaths. I believe, by the definitions I've heard, you might be the first. I'm not all that sure."

He moved the knife, waving it in an S through the air.

"She could help you."

"I don't want to be helped."

Sarah had never thought it was possible for such large men to move with such silent ease.

But Tyler and Craig had moved across the floor. Tyler was almost at her side. Craig was slightly behind Alex and to his left.

"Alex—"

"Hmm. Maybe I'm...oh, I don't know. But you know, Sarah, I think that if we'd been in high school together, you wouldn't have made fun of me. I think I will be merciful. I was merciful with Suzie. I wasn't so good to that bitchy runaway up in Sleepy Hollow. I sawed at her neck while she was alive. You—I'm going to see to it you bleed out quickly, quickly, quickly!"

"Hey, you!" Tyler called.

Stunned, Morrison swung around. He had his knife out and slashing, but it never made contact. Tyler slammed his arm down on Morrison's so hard and fast the knife went flying and the man screamed in pain.

Craig dived for the chair, spinning Sarah around, then cutting the ropes.

Sarah saw Alex Morrison was on his knees, staring up at Tyler with pure hatred.

His arm dangled at his side.

"I didn't shoot him, Craig," Tyler said. "Maybe we can get something out of him."

"After he's locked up," Craig said.

Sarah could hear sirens again.

Broken arm or not, Craig Frasier was seeing to it that Alex Morrison was handcuffed.

And Sarah was back in Tyler's arms.

"It's over," he told her as she broke into sobs. "It's truly over."

And she knew it was.

Only the nightmares would remain, and if she could wake from them in Tyler's arms, eventually, they would be over, too.

IT WAS A strange honeymoon, Tyler thought, but a great one.

The wedding, just as they had planned, took place

at Finnegan's. They'd spent a few days alone in the Poconos, and now…

Sarah had needed to see Davey, and Tyler understood. Best of all was that Sarah believed he understood.

And so…

Buzzers were ringing. Bells were chiming. Neon lights were flashing.

There really was nowhere like Vegas.

And it was great; the actual "honeymoon" part of their extended honeymoon had been personal and intimate and amazing.

And now…

Sean and Suzie had joined them. They were seeing shows, going to music events, hanging out at the hotel's stunning pool. And at night…well, they were making love in their exquisite room.

Ever since the day Tyler had rescued Sarah from Morrison, they'd planned their lives, and were living them to the fullest.

He was coming back to New York. He was going to move his investigations office there.

He could consult with police, or the FBI, since now he had some useful and friendly connections.

And Sarah would keep writing.

She was really much better than ever, she assured him. He had given her that—a greater passion for her work!

It was their last night in Vegas. Tomorrow, they'd head back and get on with their regular lives. Somehow, to Tyler, those words held a touch of magic. Real magic. They'd weathered so much.

They would continue to weather what the future might bring.

They were playing slots at the moment, because Davey loved them so much and could spend hours at a machine with a twenty-dollar bill.

Tyler was pretty sure that Davey's greatest pleasure was hitting the call button for the waitress, smiling broadly when a pretty woman brought him a Shirley Temple and then grinning toward Tyler or Sarah so that one of them would tip her.

Tyler was watching Davey when Sarah finished playing at a silly cow slot machine that said, "Moo!" every few minutes. He reached out a hand, pulling her over to sit on his lap at the stool where he'd found a place to perch.

She leaned against him. They didn't speak.

Life…

It was full of relationships. Cruel parenting had helped shape Alex Morrison. A brutal lack of empathy and lack of friendship had helped put the nails in the coffin of his psyche.

Tyler knew he'd been lucky.

He'd had a great family. And so had Sarah. And now, so close, they both had Aunt Renee and Davey.

Love was an amazing thing. There could never be too much love for many people in one's life.

And, of course, there was that one special love. Some people were lucky enough to know it when they had a chance to hold it, and hold it fast.

A forever kind of love.

Sarah was smiling at him.

He smiled back.

And it was evident, of course, but he whispered the words.

"I love you," he said.

"And I love you," she whispered back.

Davey had risen. He threw his arms around the both of them. "And I love you!" he said. "Come on, we gotta go up! Gotta get home tomorrow. I have a girlfriend, you know."

Laughing, they rose. It was time to go up to their rooms.

Tyler thought there was nothing wrong at all with a last night with Sarah in that exquisite bed!

* * * * *

Author Note

Many years ago, at a conference, I met a woman who was to become one of my best friends. She's brilliant, funny, artistic and kind. We were young, our children were young and our entire families became best friends—which we are to this day.

Connie's youngest is Josh, who has Down syndrome. He's an amazing young man. He loves the movies and everything about them, and can beat you, hands down, in any movie trivia game. He has all kinds of savvy that you might not expect. He's also a working actor, which is no easy feat. He, like his mom, is kind; there is not a mean bone in his body. I cherish his friendship and his love.

Once upon a time, I had him with me and several members of our two families at a theme park set up as a haunted attraction as Halloween approached. And while he wanted to go into one of the horror houses, Josh was afraid.

I am very easily scared myself. Truly—an absolute easy-mark coward. Therefore, it was quite simple for me to cheerfully say that I would wait with

Josh while the others went through the haunted house. But Josh saw a kiosk with some really great light-up toy swords. So we bought one, and then Josh was ready! Being brave and protective, he went ahead of me, and into the fray we charged! (Well, walked in slowly and carefully. I was—and am!—still an incredible coward!)

Actors and animatronics were everywhere.

And I couldn't help but wonder what would happen if just one little part of it all was real.

Thus this story, *Out of the Darkness*, was born!

I hope you enjoy it.

Sincerely,
Heather Graham

Turn the page for a special first look
at the next thrilling romantic suspense
in the
NEW YORK CONFIDENTIAL *series*
from New York Times *bestselling author*
Heather Graham,

A DANGEROUS GAME,

available March 13, 2018,
from MIRA Books.

Chapter 1

"Kieran, Kieran Finnegan, right?" the woman asked.

She was wrapped in a black trench coat, wore a black scarf that nearly encapsulated her face and held a dark, blanketed bundle against her chest as if it was the greatest treasure in the world.

Kieran wasn't sure when the woman had come in; the offices of psychiatrists Fuller and Miro were closed for the day, the doctors were gone and Kieran had been just about to leave herself. The reception-ist, Jake, usually locked the office door on his way out, but, apparently, tonight he had neglected to do so. Then again, Jake might have already left when Kieran's last patient had exited a little while ago.

Whether Jake had been gone or he had forgotten to lock up, the door had been left open.

And so, this woman accosted Kieran in the recep-tion area of the office just as she was on her way out.

"I am Kieran, but I'm so sorry, I'm the therapist, not one of the doctors. Actually, we are closed for the day. You'll need to come back. Both the doctors are wonderful, and I'm sure they'll be happy to see you another time."

And this woman certainly looked like she needed help.

Her eyes were huge and as dark as the clothing she was wearing as she stared at Kieran with a look of despair.

"All right, let me see what I can do. You seem distraught," Kieran said, and winced—wow. Stating the obvious. "I can get you to a hospital. I can call for help—"

"No! No!" The woman suddenly thrust the bundle she'd held so closely into Kieran's arms. "Here!"

Kieran instinctively accepted it. Reflex? She wasn't sure why.

It began to cry. And writhe. *Of course.* The bundle was a baby.

"Ma'am, please—hey!" Kieran protested.

The woman had turned and was fleeing out the door.

"Wait! Hey!" Kieran cried. She reached immediately for the phone, hoping that she'd be in time to reach the building's security desk.

Ralph Miller answered the phone at the lobby desk. "Hey, pretty girl, what are you still doing at work? I've got a few hours to go, and then I am out of here. I hear that the Danny Boys are playing at Finnegan's tonight. Can't believe your brother snagged them. I would have thought that you'd have gotten out early—"

"Ralph, listen, please! There's a woman who was

just up here. She ran out. Can you stop her from leaving the building?"

The baby wailed in earnest.

"What?"

"There's a woman in black—"

"In black, yeah. She just left."

"Stop her, catch her! Now."

"I can't hear you, Kieran. I hear a baby crying. A baby! Whose baby is it?"

"Ralph! Get out in the street and get that woman!"

"What?"

"Go catch that woman!"

"Gotcha! I'm gone."

She hung up, then quickly dialed 9-1-1.

Emergency services probably couldn't move quickly enough to help, since the woman was already on the run.

She was running on the busy streets of New York City, where rush hour meant a swarm of humanity in which one could get completely lost. But Kieran still explained her situation and where she was. The operator was efficient; cops would quickly be out. Child services would arrive.

But no matter. The woman would get away.

Kieran tried to hold and rock and soothe the baby while dialing Craig Frasier.

If you were living with an FBI agent, it made sense to call him under such circumstances, especially since he—like Ralph—would want to know why she was working so late when the Danny Boys would be playing at Finnegan's. To Craig, like Ralph, it was still a somewhat normal night—and a Friday night! A nice, normal Friday night—something that was very nice to enjoy, given their chosen professions.

"Hey, Kieran," Craig said. "Are you already at the pub?"

She apparently wasn't good at rocking and soothing and trying to talk on the phone. The baby was still crying. Loudly.

"No, I—"

"Whose kid is that? I can't hear a word you're saying!"

"I'm still at work! Can you come over here now, please?"

"Uh—yeah, sure."

Kieran hung up the phone. She didn't know what Ralph was doing; she didn't know where the police were. She glanced down at the baby as she hurried from the office, ready to hit the streets herself. How old was the tiny creature? It was so small!

Yet it had strong lungs!

Was the woman in black the mother?

She had looked older. Perhaps fifty. Too old for an infant.

Ralph wasn't at the desk; Kieran heard sirens, but, as yet, no police had arrived.

Bursting out onto the New York City street in rush hour, she looked right and left. There, far down the block, she thought she saw the woman.

"Hey!" Kieran shouted.

Despite the pulsing throng of humanity between them, the woman heard her. She turned.

There was something different about her now.

The way she moved. The way she looked; the expression on her face.

And she didn't try to run. She just stared at Kieran, and then seemed to stagger toward her.

Kieran clutched the screaming infant close to her breast and thrust her way through the people; luckily, she was a New Yorker, and she knew how to push through a crowd when necessary.

The woman was still staggering forward. Kieran was closing the gap.

"Listen, I'll help you, I'll help the baby! It's all right…"

It wasn't in any way all right.

The woman lurched forward, as if she would fall into Kieran's arms if Kieran had just been close enough.

She wasn't.

The woman fell face-first down on the sidewalk.

That was when Kieran saw the knife protruding from the woman's back and the rivulets of blood suddenly forming all around her and joining together to create a crimson pool.

Babies tended to be adorable—and this baby was especially so. In fact, Kieran wasn't sure she'd ever seen an ugly baby, but she had been assured by friends that they did exist.

This little girl, though, had a headful of auburn ringlets and huge blue eyes. Kieran had heard that all babies had blue eyes, but she didn't know if that was true or not. Sadly, she just didn't know a lot about babies; she was one in a family of four children herself, yes, but she and her twin brother, Kevin, were a couple years younger than their older brother and one year older than their younger brother.

Actually, this beautiful baby looked as if she could fit right in with their family. Each one of the Finnegan siblings had red hair and blue or green or blue-green eyes.

"They say it's the Irish," she said softly to the little one in her arms. "But I don't think that you're Irish!"

Talking to the baby made sense at the moment; FBI Special Agent Craig Frasier, the love of her life and often partner in crime—solving crime, not committing it—had arrived shortly after the police. The medical examiner had come for the body of the murdered woman and—while waiting for child services—Kieran was holding the baby, back up in the offices of Fuller and Miro.

Drs. Fuller and Miro worked with the police and other law enforcement. While not with the FBI, they were profilers and consultants for the New York office. The Bureau's behavioral-science teams were in DC, and while they could be called in, the city police and FBI often used local help in trying to get a step ahead of a criminal, or in working with criminals and witnesses when psychological assessments were needed or sometimes when a child or a distressed person simply needed to be able to speak to someone who asked the right questions and put them at ease. Kieran did a number of those assessments before reporting to the doctors, and she worked with victims of domestic abuse and both parents and children when they wound up within the child welfare system—such as a teenager who had been assaulted by her own father, or a senior who was recovering from gunshot wounds inflicted by his wife. Or Kieran's last patient today, Besa Goga. Besa was a sad case, abused for years when she'd first immigrated to the country, and now quick to strike out. Besa Goga was in court-ordered therapy because she'd bitten a man from the cable company. Kieran had only been seeing her a few weeks.

But the office didn't always work with the police department, FBI or other such agencies. They also handled other cases that fell their way through happenstance or other circumstances—like the recovering alcoholic who was also a politician and doing very well with Dr. Fuller.

Kieran had called her bosses to let them know what had happened. Both had said they'd come in immediately.

She had assured them that they must not; the police were dealing with the murder, and child services was coming for the baby.

Dr. Fuller—who had looks as dreamy as any TV physician—was at an event with his equally beautiful wife and their six-year-old.

Dr. Miro was giving a keynote speech at a conference in southern New Jersey.

Kieran had convinced them both that she was fine, that it was just strange and scary. The poor murdered woman hadn't been scary; she had touched Kieran's heart. She had needed help so badly.

But she had called Kieran by name!

And that made Kieran wonder.

She sat out in the waiting area of the offices—right where the woman had come up to her, right where the baby had been thrust into her arms. She thought that the baby was bound to cry soon. That was what babies did. They were hungry or wet or had gas or… She just really didn't have much experience. And she had no clue as to the child's age! But with little else to do—and probably in a bit of shock herself, despite the fact that she'd now thrown herself into the crime-fighting ring for a few years—she talked to the baby. She made soothing noises, discussed her own uncertainty with a cheerful voice and made a few faces.

She could swear that the baby smiled.

Did babies smile at that age?

She knew that some people—experienced parents, grandparents and so on—claimed babies did not smile until a certain age.

This one, she was certain, smiled. She waved her little fists in the air; she grinned toothlessly.

She even cooed.

"Hey!" Craig had come back up to the offices after checking out the scene on the street.

He nodded to the policeman at the door. Since Kieran had no idea what was going on, and since a woman who had been looking for her had just been stabbed to death, having a policeman standing guard was very reassuring.

She looked up at Craig, hopeful. Though, of course, she doubted that he or the police or anyone—other than the killer—knew who had just stabbed the poor woman, or why.

"You okay?" he asked her.

"I'm fine. I was handed the baby. I don't think anyone was after me for any reason at all, but…oh, Lord! Craig, you don't think it is my fault, do you? I mean, if I hadn't chased after her—"

"Kieran," he said, hunkering down by her. "No." His voice was firm and—as usual—filled with confidence and authority. Craig had been a special agent with the FBI for a good decade. He always seemed to exude a comfortable assurance and strength—things she had to admit she loved about him. Well, along with rock-hard abs, a solid six-three frame and the fact that the phrase "tall, dark and handsome" might have been conceived just for him. He had hazel eyes that were like marble, seemed to see far too much and…well, in her mind, they were just beautiful.

"It was all so fast…" Kieran murmured.

Craig adjusted the blanket around the baby. Kieran thought she cooed and smiled for him, too, but, of course, it was hard to tell.

Smile, gas. Who knew?

"Kieran, that woman was trying to save this child. She brought her to you. You aren't to blame in any way. I have a feeling that she was very heroic—and that she gave her life for the child. She might have stolen the baby from some kind of terrible situation. I don't know. None of us can even begin to figure out what might have gone down yet. But I believe the minute she took the baby away from whoever had it before, her hours were numbered." He was quiet for a moment and looked up at her. "This isn't going to be an FBI case, you know. Whoever your visitor was, she was murdered on the streets of New York. It's an NYPD matter."

"Did you talk to Ralph downstairs?" she asked anxiously. "He should have been on the desk—and you're supposed to sign in to enter this building." So it was with most large office buildings in the city. It had been ever since 9/11.

"Yes, of course, I spoke with him, the police spoke with him… He was a mess. He thinks it's all his fault. UPS was here with a large shipment for the computer-tech firm on the eighteenth floor. He thinks she slipped by him when he ran over to help the courier with the elevator," Craig said.

"I can imagine he's upset. Did he ever get out of here? He was planning on seeing the Danny Boys play tonight, too."

"I don't think he went to see the band," Craig said. "The cops let him go about an hour or so ago now."

"Ah," Kieran murmured.

What an end to the week. Ralph Miller was a Monday-to-Friday, regular-hours kind of guy. He looked forward to his Friday nights; he loved music, especially Irish rock bands. He must have been really upset to realize a murder had taken place somewhere just down the street from his front door.

The murder of a woman who had slipped by him.

A woman who had left a baby in Kieran's arms.
A baby. Alone, in her arms.

"Craig, I just… I wish I understood. And I'm not sure about the officer handling the case—"

"Kieran, no matter how long we all work in this, murder is hard to understand. That officer needed everything you could give him."

"I know that. I've spoken with him. He wants me to think. He wants me to figure out why the woman singled me out. He's more worried about that than the baby!" Kieran said indignantly.

"He's a detective, Kieran. Asking you questions is what he's supposed to do—you know that. *Can* you think of anything?" Craig asked her.

Kieran shook her head. "She probably knew about this office. And it's easy enough to find out all our names."

"Maybe, and then…"

"And then what?"

Craig smiled at her. During the diamond-heist case—when they had first met—she had saved a girl from falling onto the subway tracks when a train was coming. When a reporter had caught up with Kieran, she had impatiently said, "Anyone would lend a helping hand."

For quite some time after, she'd been a city heroine.

So she had a feeling she knew what he was going to say.

"Maybe they saw you on TV."

"That was a long time ago."

"Some people have long memories."

There was a tap at the door, and the officer who had been standing guard opened it to a stocky woman with a round face and gentle, angelic smile. She was in a uniform, and Kieran quickly realized that she was from child services.

"Hi, I'm Sandy Cleveland," the woman told her. "Child—"

"Services, yes, of course!" Kieran said.

She realized that she didn't want to hand over the baby. She didn't have a "thing" for babies—her driving goal in life had never been to get married and have children. She did want them somewhere along the line. But not now. She knew that, eventually, yes, she wanted to marry Craig. She was truly, deeply, kind-of-even-madly in love with him.

But not now. Maybe in a year. They hadn't even discussed it yet.

She didn't fawn over babies at family picnics, and she was happy for her friends who were pregnant or parents, and she got along fine with kids—little ones and big ones.

But she wasn't in any way *obsessed*.

But here, now, in the office, holding the precious little bundle, who had so recently been tenderly held by a woman who was now *dead* with a knife in her back, Kieran was suddenly loath to give her up. And not that it didn't appear the woman from child services was just about perfect for her job. No one could fake a face that held that much empathy.

"It's okay," Sandy Cleveland said very softly. "I

swear she'll be okay with me. And don't worry, we take great care of little ones at my office. I won't just dump her in a crib and let her cry. She'll be okay. It's my job—I'm very good at it," she added, as if completely aware of every bit of mixed emotion that was racing through Kieran's heart and mind. She smiled and added, "Miss Finnegan, the street below is thronging with police officers—and reporters. The chief of police is already involved in this situation. This little one will not just have the watchdogs of child services looking over her, but a guardian from the police force, as well. She's going to be fine. I personally promise you that she'll be fine."

"I'm sure—I'm sure you're good," Kieran said. She smiled at Sandy Cleveland.

"That means you have to give her the baby," Craig said, but she thought he understood, too, somehow.

"Yes, yes, of course," Kieran murmured.

And she handed over the baby.

It was so damned hard to do!

"Miss Cleveland, can you tell me about how old she is?" Kieran asked.

"I think about six weeks by her motor function. And, please, just call me Sandy," the woman told her. "Her eyes are following you—and when you speak, that's a real smile. It's usually between about six weeks and three months when they really smile, and I think this is a lovely and smart girl. Don't worry! I'll get a smile from her, too, I promise."

The baby did seem to be settling down in Sandy Cleveland's arms.

Craig set an arm around Kieran's shoulders.

"Sandy, I'm with the FBI. Craig Frasier. You won't mind if we check in on this little one?"

"Of course not!" Sandy assured them. She shook her head sadly. "I hear that the woman who handed her to you was murdered. There's no ID on her. I'm just hoping we can find out who this little one is. She's in good shape, though. Someone has been caring for her. Yes! You're so sweet!" She said the last to the baby, wrinkling her nose and making a face—and drawing a sound that wasn't quite laughter, but darned close to it. "Hopefully, she has a mom or other relatives somewhere. And if not…" She hesitated, studying Kieran and Craig. "Well, if not—a precious little infant like this? People will be jockeying to adopt her. Anyway, let me get her out of here and away from…from what happened." She held the baby adeptly while using her left hand to dig into her pocket and produce her cards. "Call me anytime," she told them. "I may not answer, but I will get back to you if you leave me a message."

Then she was gone. The cop who had been watching over Kieran went outside.

She and Craig were alone.

Kieran still felt shell-shocked.

"Kieran, hey!" Craig hunkered down by her again as she sank down into one of the comfortably upholstered chairs in the waiting room. He looked at her worriedly. "The cops are good—you know that."

"Craig, you have to be in on this. That detective—"

"Lance. Lance Kendall. Kieran, really, he's all right. He's doing all the right things."

"Yeah! All the right things—grilling me!"

"All right, I will speak with Egan about it tomorrow, how's that?"

She nodded. "Thank you. Get one of your joint task forces going—at least maybe you can participate?"

"Sure." He hesitated. "I guess... Um, well."

There was a tap at the door. They both looked up. Craig stood.

A man walked in. It wasn't the first officer who had arrived at the scene—it was the detective who had arrived while others were setting up crime scene tape around parameters, handling the rush-hour crowd around the body and urging her to get the baby back up to her offices—out of the street.

He was a tall, well-built African American man. About six feet even, short brown hair, light brown eyes and features put together correctly. He was around forty-five, she thought. He wasn't warm and cuddly, but neither was he rude.

"Detective Kendall," Craig said. "Have you wrapped up at the scene for the evening?"

"Yes—a few techs are still down there, but there's nothing more I can accomplish here. Unless you can help. Miss Finnegan—nothing? You can't think of anything?"

"I have no idea why this lady chose me," Kieran said. "None."

"And you've never seen the woman before?" Kendall asked.

"Never."

"Nor the baby?"

Did he think that the infant paid social calls on people, hung out at the pub or requested help from psychiatrists or a psychologist?

"No," she managed evenly. "I've never seen the infant before. I've never seen the woman before."

"All right, then." He suddenly softened, becoming a little warmer. "You must be really shaken. I understand that, and I'm sorry. For now, I don't have anything else. But, of course, I'm sure you know we may need to question you again."

"I'm not leaving town," she said drily.

He wasn't amused.

Kieran continued, "And, of course, I've spoken with both Dr. Fuller and Dr. Miro. I've told them all that I could, and they will be trying to think of any reason—other than who they are and what they do—that the woman might have come here."

"I've spoken with Drs. Fuller and Miro, too," Detective Kendall told her grimly. "And I'm sure we'll speak again."

"I'm sure," Kieran murmured.

"Good night, Special Agent Frasier, Miss Finnegan," the detective said. "You're both—uh, free to go."

He left them. Craig pulled Kieran around and into his arms, looking down into her eyes. "We are free.

There's nothing else to do tonight. You want to go home?"

"I know that we both really wanted to see the band play tonight," she told him. "I'm sorry."

"Kieran, it's not your fault—I'm sure you didn't plan for a woman to thrust a baby into your arms and then run downstairs and be stabbed to death."

"It's driving me crazy, Craig! We don't know who she was… We don't have a name for her, we don't know about the baby. I think she was too old to be the mom, but I'm not really sure. And if not…she was trying to save the baby, not hurt it. But who would hurt a baby?"

"I don't know. Let's get on home, shall we?"

"We can still go to the pub. Maybe catch the last of the Danny Boys?" she said.

"You know you don't want to go anywhere."

Kieran hesitated. "Not true. I do want to go somewhere. I'm starving—and I'm not sure what we've got to eat at the apartment."

"Yep. We've been staying at yours—if there is food at mine, I'm certain we don't want to eat it."

"Then we'll go to the pub," she said quietly.

Kieran hadn't realized just how late it had grown until she and Craig walked out of the building. New York City policemen were still busy on the street, many of them just managing crowd control; the body of the murdered woman was gone, but crime scene workers were still putting the pieces together of what might and might not be a clue on the busy street.

They were in midtown, with giant conglomerates mixed with smaller boutiques and shops. Most of the shops were closed and the hour too late for business, but people still walked quickly along the sidewalks, slowing down curiously to watch the police and try to see what had happened. Kieran looked up while Craig spoke with a young policewoman for a moment; her brother had once warned her that she looked up too often—that she looked like a tourist.

But she loved even the rooftops, the skyline. Old skyscrapers with ornate molding at the roof sat alongside new giants that towered above them in glass, chrome and steel. And then again, right in the midst of the twentieth- and twenty-first-century buildings, there would be a charming throwback to the 1800s.

From a nearby Chinese restaurant, a tempting aroma laced the air.

Even over murder.

The cops generally knew Craig; he was polite to all of them, as well. They nodded an acknowledgment to Kieran. She'd worked with the police often enough herself.

"Is Detective McBride going to be on the case?" Kieran asked hopefully. They'd worked with McBride before, not even a year ago, and he had been an amazing ally.

Doctors Fuller and Miro worked with city detectives regularly, and—nine out of ten—they were great. Every once in a while, as in any job, there was a total jerk in the mix. Mainly they were professionals, and good at their work, and Kieran knew it. Some were more personable than others. Homicide detectives could be very cut-and-dried. McBride had told her once that homicide, while horrible, was also easier than dealing with other crimes. The victims couldn't complain about the way he was working. Of course, the victims had relatives. That was hard.

She had come to really like McBride.

In this case, a baby was involved. A woman had died trying to save that baby, Kieran was certain. So she felt they needed the best.

Craig looked at her quizzically. "You know that that there are thousands of detectives in the city, a decent percentage of that in Homicide—and even a decent percentage in Major Case."

"Actually, when you break it all down..."

"I don't know who will be working the case— probably more than one detective. But, for right now, it is Lance Kendall. And he's all right, Kieran. He's good. He was doing all the right things," he added quietly. He looked as if he was going to say something more. He didn't.

He took her hand in his. She held on, letting the warmth of his touch comfort her as they walked down the street. "Hey, remember. I'm an agent. You work with psychiatrists who spend most of their time on criminal cases. It's a life we've chosen, and we've talked about it. This will be just another case—whatever level of involvement we have with it. You can't let it take over— or neither one of us will be sane."

She nodded. He was right. There were other cases where they found themselves on the fringe; and, frankly, every day of Craig's life had to do with criminal activity in the city of New York. They'd already worked on cases of cruel and brutal murders. This was another. And there was always something that seemed to make it better—at least for the survivors—when a killer was brought to justice.

She couldn't obsess. She knew it.

But this one felt personal!

"Yep," she spoke blithely and smiled.

"You're cool?" He didn't believe her, she could tell; it seemed he didn't know whether to push it or not.

But he was right about one thing. There was nothing for them to do right now except try to get their minds around what had happened—and let it go enough to get on with life.

Even figure out how to step back in order to step forward again.

"Yep. I'm fine. Let's get food," Kieran said.

"Sounds good. Thankfully, we always know where to go!"

Follow Kieran Finnegan and
Special Agent Craig Frasier
as they investigate.
Who was the woman?
Where did the baby come from?
Can Kieran stay out of trouble when a lead
surfaces through the family pub?

A DANGEROUS GAME
by Heather Graham.

Available March 13, 2018,
from MIRA Books.

Get 2 Free Books,
Plus 2 Free Gifts—
just for trying the Reader Service!

HARLEQUIN
INTRIGUE

SPECIAL EXCERPT FROM

*Lawson Granger thought he put his past behind him...
until his first love, Eve Cooper, returns to Wrangler's
Creek, Texas, with a baby on the way and a teenage
daughter with questions about her real father...*

*Enjoy a sneak peek of TEXAS-SIZED TROUBLE,
part of the **A WRANGLER'S CREEK NOVEL** series
by USA TODAY bestselling author Delores Fossen.*

She was dying. Eve was sure of it.

The pain was knifing through her, and the contractions were so powerful that it felt as if King Kong were squeezing her belly with his hairy fist. Her breathing was too fast. Her heart racing.

And now she was hallucinating.

Either that or Lawson Granger had indeed slipped in the puddle where her water had broken and was now dying from a head injury. Great. If it wasn't a hallucination, it meant she'd returned to Wrangler's Creek after all these years only to cause the death of her old flame.

Her old flame grunted, cursed and maneuvered himself onto all fours. So, not dead, just perhaps with critical internal injuries. Of course, anything she was thinking or considering right now could be blown out of proportion because of the god-awful pain that was vising her stomach.

"My water broke," she managed to say. "And my phone." She'd dropped it when one of the contractions had hit, and the phone was now scattered all over the stone entryway and hardwood floor.

Eve wouldn't mention that the reason her water had broken right by the door was because she'd been trying to hear who was talking outside the guesthouse. She'd thought it was another of her *fans*. Apparently not though.

"This is too soon," she muttered. "I'm not due for three and a half weeks. A baby shouldn't come this soon, should it?" Eve knew she sounded frantic, perhaps even crazy, but she couldn't make herself stop babbling. "Please tell me the baby will be all right."

Lawson lifted his head, making eye contact with her. Yes, he possibly did have a head injury because he looked dazed.

Oh, God. There was blood.

It was on his head and on the butt of his jeans. Eve saw it while he was still on all fours and trying to get to his feet.

"You're hurt," she said, but it was garbled because another contraction hit her. For this one, King Kong had brought one of his friends to help him squeeze her belly. Because Eve had no choice; she dropped to the floor.

She was sinking onto her knees just as Lawson was getting to his. He caught on to the wall and, grunting and making sounds of pain, he got to his feet. He glanced around as if trying to get his bearings, and he growled out more of that profanity. Some of it had her name in the mix. It definitely wasn't the sweet tone he'd used when they were teenagers and he'd charmed her out of her underpants.

Where will this unexpected reunion lead?
Find out in TEXAS-SIZED TROUBLE by
USA TODAY *bestselling author Delores Fossen, available now.*

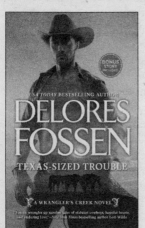

$7.99 U.S./$9.99 CAN.